D0473545

THE SHOOTING SCRIPT

™

MERLIN

MERLIN

TELEPLAY BY
DAVID STEVENS AND PETER BARNES
STORY BY
ED KHMARA

FOREWORD BY
ROBERT HALMI, SR.

A Newmarket Shooting Script™ Series Book
NEWMARKET PRESS • NEW YORK

Copyright © 1998 by Hallmark Entertainment

All interior photographs by Oliver Upton

This book is published simultaneously in the United States of America and in Canada.

All rights reserved. This book may not be reproduced, in whole, or in part, in any form, without written permission.
Inquiries should be addressed to Permissions Department,
Newmarket Press, 18 East 48th Street, New York, New York 10017.

10 9 8 7 6 5 4

Library of Congress Cataloging in Publication Data available upon request

ISBN 1-55704-366-3

QUANTITY PURCHASES
Companies, professional groups, clubs, and other organizations
may qualify for special terms when ordering quantities of this title.
For information, write Special Sales, Newmarket Press,
18 East 48th Street, Suite 1501, New York, New York 10017,
call (212) 832-3575, or fax (212) 832-3629.

Manufactured in the United States of America

CONTENTS

FOREWORD

BY ROBERT HALMI, SR.

Bringing Merlin to the screen represents a great challenge, but also the possibility of great reward. The challenge is successfully marrying myth, literature and fantasy. But if that's done right, the payoff will be enormous. We'll have four hours of mass entertainment that will tell a great story, that will be visually stunning, and that will be truly memorable.

Merlin, above all, is great entertainment. It takes us back to a time when morality mattered, when "doing the right thing" was more than just a cliché. Its themes are grand and ultimately life-affirming, its landscape vast and colorful. We all know at least snippets of this huge saga—Camelot, Excalibur, King Arthur, for example—but this script, using Merlin/Nimue as its central story arc, provides a coherent whole. And the Mab/Frik/Morgan dynamic adds a glorious amount of delicious wit and humor.

This story could not be told in a two-hour feature film. It *demands* more time. Television's miniseries format is perfect for something this big.

Gulliver's Travels, with Ted Danson and Mary Steenburgen, marked Hallmark Entertainment's first miniseries outing with NBC, and it was a major critical and ratings success. We loved working with Don Ohlmeyer, Lindy DeKoven, Gary Kessler and their creative, marketing, and publicity teams. They not only understood our company's goal of transforming classic literature into top-rate entertainment, they made it their goal, too!

They're not meddlers, they're contributors, collaborators. They understand that to break through the clutter of today's noisy and jammed television landscape, you have to do something that's *big*, something that says "quality," something that stands out in the madding, heavily-cloned program crowd. My hat is off to our colleagues at NBC, who are leaders.

Our second big project for NBC was *The Odyssey,* with Armand Assante, Greta Scacchi, Isabella Rossellini, Vanessa Williams, Eric Roberts and Bernadette Peters. Again, success.

On April 26 and 27, 1998, we up the ante with *Merlin.* A cast this large and rich in talent is almost unprecedented: Sam Neill, Isabella Rossellini, Martin Short, Miranda Richardson, Sir John Gielgud, Helena Bonham Carter, Rutger Hauer, James Earl Jones, Billie Whitelaw—the list just goes on and on. Steve Barron directs from a smart (and often very funny) script by Ed Khmara and David Stevens. Peter Barnes' contributions were considerable.

It's interesting, I think, that we could not have made this *Merlin* even six months ago, or at least could not have made it as exciting and visually enthralling as it is. That's because almost every month some new special effects (CGI) techniques are perfected, and we use them all! *Gulliver's Travels* had 125 special effects; *The Odyssey* had just over 200. *Merlin* employs special effects in 450 places! It's remarkable how our ability to tell a story is enhanced by state-of-the-art CGI technology, perfected by our friends at FrameStore in London.

I should also acknowledge the hard-working geniuses at the Jim Henson Creature Shop. They helped us make the unreal seem real.

Virtually all our upcoming productions—*Moby Dick* (with Patrick Stewart and Gregory Peck), *Noah's Ark, Crime and Punishment, Animal Farm, Huckleberry Finn, David Copperfield* and many, many more—will be enriched by CGI, but those effects must always be seen in the context of a means to an end. And the "end" is to tell an engaging story in a clear and entertaining way, a story that will seize the mind and imagination of tens of millions of intelligent viewers.

I believe *Merlin*—with all its evocative themes of myth and magic—will once again entertain (and hopefully inform) Americans. I'm pleased—thanks to this book—that readers will have an opportunity to examine the material upon which it is based. Our cast is brilliant, the direction is inspired, the crew worked their hearts out to make this picture, the special effects are stunning—but in the pages that follow, you can see where it all started, what kept us all on course, and what served as our inspiration.

Enjoy!

SYNOPSIS

PART ONE

"Hark, now hear the sailors cry
Smell the sea and feel the sky
Let your soul and spirit fly
into the mystic..."

Before Excalibur, before the Knights of the Round Table, before Arthur, Guinevere, Lancelot and Galahad, there was a sorcerer shrouded in the mists...and this is his tale.

As the voice of an elderly wizard tells of a time long ago, we open on Merlin *(Sam Neill)*, astride his faithful steed, Sir Rupert, making his annual pilgrimage to Avalon Abbey. Father Abbot *(Timothy Bateson)*, master of the Avalon Abbey, takes Merlin to visit his lost love, Nimue *(Isabella Rossellini)*, whose veiled face reveals little, but whose eyes speak of a pure and eternal love. "Nimue," says Merlin, "You are my sunlight...without you I'm lost."

Merlin tells Nimue of Arthur *(Paul Curran)*, a man he believes to be of pure heart, "golden, fine, handsome—everything I dreamed he'd be." Arthur had brought Merlin important news: King Uther is dead. Merlin, of course, already knew, and told the startled young man that now he, Arthur, would become king. Why? Because he was born to it. Because Uther was his father.

And so, the old wizard recounts the old times...the bloody times...the terrible times...

King Constant *(John Gielgud)*, Arthur's grandfather, was the first Christian king of England. King Constant was a good man, who later became a tyrant. During his final battle he screams at the leader of the victorious opposing forces, Vortigern *(Rutger Hauer)*, "My son, Uther, will avenge me. You'll never sleep easy, knowing he'll come for you, Vortigern!" As King Constant is beheaded, the crown of England rolls across the floor to Vortigern, who puts it upon his head.

Thus began a calamitous civil war which tore the country apart. Christian churches are destroyed and defiled, as are the sacred places of the old pagan religion.

The country and its people drown in blood. A dying woman begs Queen Mab *(Miranda Richardson)*—a darkly beautiful woman, powerful and charismatic—to help end the bloodshed. At first, Mab demurs. "I can't. Too many people have forsaken the Old Ways and become Christian . . . I no longer have the power." The old woman pushes her to help. "Save us, and the people will come back to you, and the peace they lost when they forsook you." Mab makes a commitment: "I will save them, and the Old Ways. I swear it!"

Mab informs her sister, the beautiful, fair-haired Lady of the Lake *(Miranda Richardson)*, of her momentous decision. "I'm going to create a leader for the people," Mab declares. "A powerful wizard who'll save Britain and bring back the people to us and the Old Ways."

The Lady of the Lake cautions her sister to be wary, that her task may drain what powers she still has. Mab, however, vows to fight on, telling her sister that if people stop believing in the old ways, Mab and her kind will cease to exist.

Mab conjures Merlin out of a dazzling array of colored crystals. Frik *(Martin Short)*, her gnome-like manservant, watches awe-struck.

Thus is Merlin born, to Elissa *(Emma Lewis)*—whom Mab subsequently abandons to die. "She'd served her purpose," she haughtily tells Ambrosia *(Billie Whitelaw)*, a former follower of Mab who's been drafted to raise Merlin into adulthood.

Why can't Mab herself raise Merlin? Because, explains the tart-tongued Ambrosia, "You need more than tricks to bring up a child. You need patience, understanding, and love. Above all, you need *love*. That's something you had once but have no more."

Mab's retort is brief and chilling. "Remember, he's only half-human, and he belongs to me. He's my son! I'll send for him when it's time."

When he's seventeen, Merlin encounters the beautiful Nimue, daughter of Lord Ardent *(John McEnery)*. It's love at first sight. When, on a journey, she sinks into a treacherous mudhole, Merlin for the first time becomes aware of the special power with which he has been blessed/cursed. He holds out a branch for her to grasp, to save herself. It is not long enough. He wills it to grow. It does. Merlin returns to Ambrosia's cottage and announces breathlessly, "I've seen her! The most beautiful girl in the world. We'll love each other always!"

For Ambrosia, the news is bittersweet. Merlin's having exercised his special power means the moment she's been dreading since Merlin was born and she became his surrogate mother has arrived. It's time for him to leave. A golden horse materializes to take Merlin away. Ambrosia's parting words will haunt him forever: "Magic has no power over the human heart. Don't forget what I taught you! Never stop fighting for what's right."

Frik guides Merlin to Queen Mab, who announces to the assembled throng of fairies and elves, "This is Merlin, who comes to save us. He will bring the people back to the Old Ways!" She tells Merlin that she will teach him to become the most powerful wizard the world has ever known. The "schooling" doesn't go smoothly. As Frik, now the pedantic schoolmaster, informs Mab, "In his heart he [Merlin] doesn't like magic. The truth is he wants to go home."

And he does. Merlin becomes a teenage runaway, much to Mab's disgust. "He's on his way home to that viper-tongued witch, Ambrosia," she fumes.

When he reaches Ambrosia's cottage, Ambrosia's all but dead. She is able, however, to issue this final injunction to young Merlin: "Remember, only listen to your heart..."

She dies. Merlin vents his rage on Mab: "You killed her like you killed my real mother!" "No," Mab responds. "I only let her die. I'm sorry about your mother and Ambrosia, but they were casualties of war. I'm fighting to save my people from extinction."

Over the grave of the beloved Ambrosia, Merlin declares, "I'll only ever use my powers to defeat Queen Mab, never to help her...this I swear."

Nimue, meanwhile, grows into a stunningly beautiful woman. We next encounter her when she's with her father, Lord Ardent, a fawning courtier at Vortigern's campsite. Vortigern is nervous about Ardent's loyalty to him; he suspects Ardent's real attachment is to his archenemy, Prince Uther *(Mark Jax)*. Vortigern announces he's taking Ardent's daughter, Nimue, hostage. "Stay loyal to me, and she'll be returned to you, safe and sound. Join Uther and I'll kill her."

Vortigern is having an impossible time trying to build a tower for his new castle. It keeps collapsing. Merlin is drafted to lend his special talent to the exercise. While doing so, he has a vision: two dragons, one red, one white. The white one represents Vortigern, the red one, Prince Uther. In Merlin's imagination, the red dragon triumphs.

Vortigern is in awe of Merlin's power. Forewarned about Uther's strategy, he can act accordingly, and decisively. He acknowledges Merlin's extraordinary gifts, but ever fearful of betrayal, tosses Merlin into prison.

In jail, Merlin is reunited with his beloved Nimue. Nimue asks him what he wants. "I'd like to see England at peace, an England of kindness and chivalry," Merlin responds. "An England where men and women could live secure, without hatred or envy, where misery was unknown and happiness was for all."

"That's a vision we both share," Nimue tells Merlin. She also tells Merlin about an island called Avalon, home of the Holy Grail, a cup that has the power to feed the hungry and heal the sick. Since biblical times, she says, many men have searched for it, but no one has seen it. "But one day a man with a pure heart will find it and peace and happiness will return."

Mab, meanwhile, is up to her old, manipulative ways. She tells Vortigern she'll help him defeat Uther if he (Vortigern) will deliver Merlin unto her. She tells Vortigern that the key to defeating Uther is to sacrifice Nimue to the Great Dragon. Especially after Vortigern learns that Nimue's father, Lord Ardent, has defected and joined Prince Uther's cause, Vortigern enthusiastically agrees to Mab's vicious scheme.

In spite of Merlin's superhuman efforts to save her from the omnipowerful dragon, Nimue is badly burned by the rampaging, fire-breathing giant. Merlin takes the injured Nimue to Avalon. The nuns of the great abbey use their knowledge of ancient herbs and potions to try to save Nimue's life.

Merlin, meanwhile, is furious. "You destroyed everyone I love," he screams at Mab, "my mother, Ambrosia . . . and now Nimue."

"The end justifies the means," she cooly responds. "I did it for you. I want you to use the power in you. Rise up, dear, dear Merlin and *be great!*"

After vowing to destroy her, Merlin consults with Mab's sister, the Lady of the Lake. He tells her he needs a great sword to kill Vortigern, whom he describes as "a bad king and Mab's friend." She gives him Excalibur!

At Winchester Castle, Merlin meets with Prince Uther, his knights and lords—including the big, blustering Sir Boris *(Roger Ashton-Griffiths)* and the cool, detached Duke of Cornwall *(Thomas Lockyer)*. Merlin tells Uther that Vortigern plans an immediate attack. Why, Uther wonders out loud, is Merlin helping him? Because Vortigern is the friend of his enemy (Mab), Merlin explains, "so the enemy of my enemy is my friend. Besides, I've seen the Red Dragon defeat the White and I think you might make a fair to decent king."

A thunderous battle ensues, with brutal, hand-to-hand fighting, in appalling conditions. As foretold, Lord Ardent, Nimue's father, allies himself with Uther. Vortigern and Merlin have a titanic encounter. Merlin uses Excalibur to dispatch the evil Vortigern.

Merlin thinks good has triumphed. "I thought Uther would be a good king and so help defeat Mab," he later reflects. "But I was never a good judge of men. I always expected too much of them . . ."

At Winchester's Pendragon Castle, the Duke of Cornwall presents his beautiful wife, Igraine *(Rachel Clover)*, and his daughter Morgan Le Fey *(Helena Bonham Carter)*, to newly-installed King Uther. Uther is overwhelmed by Igraine's beauty; his carnal desires are apparent. He tells Merlin, "I want her more than I've ever wanted anything in the world."

"How great is your power?" he asks Merlin. "Can you make a woman love me?" No, says Merlin. "Magic can't create love." Uther reminds Merlin that he (Uther) has Excalibur. Merlin offers to make a spell; Uther gives Excalibur to him; Merlin—in one swift movement—drives it into a rock, thereby waking the Mountain King *(James Earl Jones)*. Merlin asks the Mountain King to be the caretaker of Excalibur, "until a good man takes it from you."

Uther tries to extricate Excalibur from the rock. Of course, his attempt fails.

Uther lays siege to the Duke of Cornwall at Tintagel Castle. Months pass. As Sir Boris reminds Uther, "The kingdom is falling apart while we tear ourselves to pieces." And, he adds incredulously, "All this for a woman?!"

Much to Uther's surprise, Merlin offers to help Uther bed Lady Igraine, as long as Igraine's husband, the Duke of Cornwall, isn't harmed. Why would the virtuous Merlin back such an adulterous plot? Because, he says, Uther and Igraine will have a child, a boy—and that child will be Merlin's! "What'll you do with him?" Uther asks. "Teach him honor and goodness," Merlin responds.

When Cornwall leaves Tintagel one evening, Merlin transforms Uther into Cornwall. The castle guards, not knowing of the duplicity, permit Uther-as-Cornwall to reenter the grounds. Uther-as-Cornwall has his way with Igraine; not-so-little and plenty-nasty Morgan Le Fey knows exactly what's up.

Cornwall—the *real* Cornwall—is killed by Uther's men, even though letting him live was a condition of Merlin's helping Uther.

As predicted, Igraine gives birth to Arthur. "At last," Merlin exults, "a good man, a good king!" As always, the perpetually-scheming Mab deflates his expectations. "You're easily fooled," she tells Merlin. "Uther's child is damned. He did it when he killed Cornwall. Arthur will be his father's son! Because of him, the chaos of blood will go on and on and out of it the people come back to me!"

Mab's chameleon-like toady, Frik, gives Morgan Le Fey a rune stone, and has her hide the stone in the baby's crib.

PART TWO

Merlin tutors the young Arthur. "I didn't teach him magic," Merlin later remembers. "I taught him ethics, morals—which is much more difficult, believe me..."

They ride to Excalibur village, where a whole village has sprung up 'round the sword in the rock. Arthur confides to Merlin that he wants to be king. "I'd do the things you taught me," he tells Merlin. "Build a golden city called Camelot, devoted to peace and charity."

As Arthur grasps the sword, the face of the Mountain King appears in the rock. Arthur identifies himself as the only son of Uther (who, shamed over the death of Cornwall, committed suicide), "and the rightful king of Britain."

Mab urges the Mountain King not to give Excalibur to Arthur. "He'll betray the people, just as his father did," she says. The Mountain King decrees that the boy has a good heart, and permits Arthur to extract Excalibur from the rock. Blood drips from his hands as Arthur pulls the red-hot sword from the stone. Mab declares ominously, "His reign begins in blood and will end the same way."

Arthur is crowned king, although powerful Lord Lot *(John Turner)* refuses to recognize him as such. Lot's son, Gawain *(Sebastian Roche)*, however, does swear allegiance to Arthur. Peace is eventually obtained when Arthur is magnanimous on the battlefield. "You are the true king," Lord Lot declares.

Meanwhile, Frik—acting, as always, at the behest of Mab—goes to work on Morgan Le Fey, transforming her into a vision of beauty. The Mab/Frik grand plan? Perhaps if Morgan Le Fey had a son, *he* could become king! Frik introduces the nefarious Morgan (who takes on the bogus title of Lady Marie, Queen of the Border Celts) to King Arthur, who, not knowing she is his half-sister, is smitten by her.

Merlin, unaware of Mab's machinations and believing his work is done, retires to Avalon to be with his beloved Nimue. But as he sits beside the sleeping Nimue he sees the ghastly, obscene image of Arthur and Morgan Le Fey making love. Merlin races to Pendragon Castle and confronts Arthur, who admits everything. Merlin utters a dreadful prediction: "There will be a child. Mab will see to that. He'll be the future, and he'll destroy us."

The unrelenting Mab goes to work on another front. She allows Nimue to see a tantalizing image of herself *without* scars, her beauty restored. Mab makes her an offer: "I'll restore your beauty permanently if you'll take Merlin away to a place I've created for you. You can live with him there until the end of your days."

Nimue says she can't accept the offer; it would mean Merlin would have to abandon his cause.

The city of Camelot is being built, on a beautiful site of rolling hills and glorious countryside. Arthur announces to Merlin that he's going to marry Guinevere *(Lena Heady)*, Lord Leo's *(Nicholas Clay)* daughter. Merlin presents the bride with a tiny wooden table, with roots like a tree. "It's a perfect circle," he tells Arthur. "If you plant it in Camelot it will grow. It will come to symbolize everything we stand for..." For his part, Arthur vows to atone for his sinning with Morgan. "One day," he declares, "I'll find the Holy Grail."

The years pass. At Camelot, it seems that Guinevere has brought the priceless gift of happiness.

But all good things must end, or so it seems.

Merlin begs Morgan Le Fey not to teach her hell-on-wheels young son Mordred (fathered by Arthur) the Old Ways. She haughtily refuses his request. Mab, meanwhile, is besotted with the little brat. "You'll be the death of Arthur," she coos to the wretched child, "and the end of all of Merlin's dreams...won't you, my sweetest?"

Merlin explains to Mab's benevolent sister, the Lady of the Lake, that he has to find a man to guard the throne when Arthur goes searching for the Holy Grail. "You need a man pure in heart," says the Lady, and offers to take Merlin by ship to Joyous Gard. That's where Merlin finds Galahad *(Justin Girdler)*, son of Lady Elaine *(Janine Eser)*, and Lancelot *(Jeremy Sheffield)*—"a charismatic figure, perhaps a little too handsome and certainly a little too complacent." Merlin explains that he's come to find a man to defend King Arthur in his kingdom. Lancelot agrees to embark upon what his wife describes as "one last great adventure."

Back at Camelot, Lancelot defeats Gawain in a jousting tournament; by so doing, he wins the right to serve as protector of Guinevere's virtue while Arthur is away searching for the Holy Grail.

And then it all falls apart. Mab, of course, is the force masterminding the chaos.

Lancelot falls in love with Guinevere. Mab makes sure Lancelot's wife, Elaine, witnesses the act of unfaithfulness. Elaine dies of a broken heart.

Nimue makes a pact with the devil (er, Mab). Nimue agrees to go to a faraway place, from which she can never return, if Merlin will come to her there. Mab promises her he will.

Mab wrests Mordred from his mother, Morgan Le Fey, who subsequently dies after "slipping" on some stairs. Frik has lost his beloved; he secretly turns against Mab at that moment.

Arthur eventually returns, *sans* the Grail. Mordred ("I'm your long lost son, Father," he intones) confronts Arthur with the fact of Guinevere's adultery. He and many knights, including Sir Boris, demand the death penalty for her treason. She is to be burned at the stake. But just as the flames around her take hold, Merlin causes a sudden cloudburst; the flames around the stake are doused. Lancelot cuts Guinevere free, pulls her onto his horse and they gallop away.

Merlin and Arthur have conspired to permit the rescue. Merlin describes Arthur's gesture as an act of love.

Finally, Merlin and Nimue are reunited, in peace, in the enchanted cavern—which, it turns out, is in the forest around Ambrosia's cottage where he spent his childhood. "This is what I've always dreamed of . . ." Merlin declares, as Nimue points to her unscarred face, and they embrace. Their rapture is interrupted, though, as Merlin intuits what is happening a world away in Salisbury Plain, where Arthur and his allies, including Gawain, Sir Boris—and Frik!—are locked in fierce battle with Mordred. Mordred kills Gawain's father, Lord Lot, and almost kills Gawain.

The fight is long and bloody. Arthur, armed with Excalibur, is ready to dispatch Mordred when the weasel utters these pathetic words, "Father, another sin? You'd kill your own son?" During the split second Arthur's mental attention is diverted, Mordred stabs him. Arthur staggers and, in a fury, turns on Mordred and runs him through. Arthur falls, mortally wounded.

Merlin tells Nimue he must be by the dying Arthur's side. "I have to do this, Nimue, or I wouldn't be the man you love," he declares. Nimue makes the supreme sacrifice—knowing that if he leaves, Merlin can never return to the enchanted cave or to her. She urges him to go quickly.

Arthur dies. A grief-stricken Merlin rushes to the water's edge and hurls Excalibur high into the air. "You lied to me," he tells the Lady of the Lake. No, she says, "I told you the answer was at Joyous Gard."

Merlin suddenly (and far too late) realizes the protector, the man with the pure heart, was never Lancelot. It was the boy, Galahad.

When Mordred dies, Mab swears to make the whole world pay for her loss.

The last great battle—Mab vs. Merlin—is joined. Mab throws swirling bursts of fire at him; each one is parried by Merlin. He refuses to retaliate. He just lets Mab expend her waning powers. When Mab unleashes a mighty torrent of water, Merlin freezes it before it can hit him.

Merlin's ultimate strategy? "We're going to forget you, Mab." And with that, Merlin, Frik, Gawain—and the whole army—simply turn their backs on Mab. "You can't fight us or frighten us," he tells her. "You're just not important enough anymore. We forget you, Queen Mab. Go join your sister in the lake and be forgotten."

Galahad rides through the winter landscape, carrying the Holy Grail, a silver cup that shines with a strange light.

Old Merlin is recounting the story to us: "And he brought with him the Holy Grail . . . and Spring, and the land became fertile again and the cycle of darkness and death ended . . . "

And what of Merlin and his beloved? Well, Merlin learns from Frik that after Mab's spells began to lose their power, Nimue found herself free. Ever since, she's been searching for Merlin. Eventually, they find each other. Merlin has one trick left, and only one. He makes them young again!

As they walk away, Merlin tells her, "There's no more . . . that's the end of magic!"

Above: Let the joust begin!

Merlin

Screenplay by
Ed Khmara and David Stevens*

*Pending WGA arbitration

<u>INSERT</u>

1. <u>CLOSE SHOT: OLD MERLIN.</u> This is the MERLIN we all know from legend - a wise old wizard with a long white beard, gentle but piercing eyes and with a traditional conical hat. He looks STRAIGHT AT CAMERA.

> OLD MERLIN:
> (urgently)
> Listen! Once upon a time ... No, that's not the way to start, you'll think this is a fairy-tale and it isn't. It has elements of a fairy-story, dragons, elves, fairies and such ... and it has magic. But in my time magic was much more commonplace ... Well, well, all things change ... the arrow of time points in one direction ... So, where should I begin? It's obvious I should start at the beginning but I've never done the obvious, so I'll start in the middle and work my way back to the beginning!
> (he gives a dry chuckle)

2. <u>EXT. SURFACE OF THE SUN. DAY.</u>

Gigantic flames leap from the sun. Beautiful tentacles of flame lick the universe.

They seem to dance joyfully, bringing life to the world.

> OLD MERLIN'S VOICE:
> It was Spring and I was on my way to Avalon ...

3. <u>EXT. COUNTRYSIDE. DAY.</u>

The sun burns in the sky as MERLIN rides across the countryside.

> OLD MERLIN'S VOICE:
> I went to Avalon every year ...

<u>CLOSE SHOT: MERLIN.</u> The 40 year old MERLIN wipes off the horse's sweat with a cloth.

> MERLIN:
> It's hot today, Rupert.
> (he seems to be talking to himself)
> You're being very rude, not answering. It's the height of bad manners, Rupert.

There is a dismissive, blowing sound.

RUPERT'S VOICE:
I don't need you to instruct me in manners, good or bad, sir …

MERLIN:
I'm glad you're speaking to me at last, Rupert.

CAMERA BACK to show it is the horse, RUPERT who is talking in a very upper class accent.

RUPERT:
<u>Sir</u> Rupert, if you please. I was named Sir Rupert, sired by Prince Thunder, out of Joanna the Bold …

MERLIN:
Fine stock, Sir Rupert, fine stock.

RUPERT is mollified by MERLIN's remark.

RUPERT:
The finest … If I was a little distracted, I apologise, Merlin. It's the smithy in Salisbury, he's done an extremely bad job on my shoes. They hurt terribly.

MERLIN:
Oh dear, I'm sorry Sir Rupert.

RUPERT:
You can't get good craftsmen nowadays … no pride in their work.

MERLIN:
I agree … If your shoes're hurting so, Sir Rupert, I think we should hurry. The sooner we get to Avalon, the sooner you can rest.

RUPERT:
You're right.

RUPERT breaks into a gallop. MERLIN smiles, he has neatly let the horse talk itself into going faster.

4. <u>EXT. AVALON ABBEY. DAY.</u>

The abbey sits in the centre of an island with a tidal causeway approaching it.
As MERLIN dismounts the small, jolly, middle-aged FATHER ABBOT rushes
out to greet him - and rushes straight past him. The FATHER ABBOT is very
very short-sighted. He addresses the HORSE.

                    FATHER ABBOT:
          Merlin! It's been so long.

                    MERLIN:
          I'm here, Father.
                    FATHER ABBOT:
                    (whirling round)
          What?! What? What?! Oh yes! …

The two OLD FRIENDS embrace and walk towards the entrance to the Abbey.

                    MERLIN:
          Could you take care of Sir Rupert?

                    FATHER ABBOT:
                    (peering round)
          Where is he?

MERLIN indicates the HORSE following behind them.

                    MERLIN:
          He's there …

FATHER ABBOT turns and peers closely at the HORSE.

                    FATHER ABBOT:
          Yes, yes … of course … You know, monks say my eyesight's
          getting worse. I pay them no heed, it's the sort of rumour and
          gossip that's bound to arise in a closed community like ours.

MERLIN nods sagely, determined to humour his old FRIEND.

                    MERLIN:
                    (sympathetically)
          You're right … Quite … quite …

5.   <u>INT. AVALON ABBEY. DAY</u>

The vaulted arches of the Abbey soar into the darkness. Candles cast a dim light. Some NUNS are praying whilst others chant gently.

FATHER ABBOT comes in with MERLIN. The FATHER genuflects before the alter. MERLIN, pointedly, does not. Instead he moves to a dark corner where there is a wooden screen with a carved grille.

6.   <u>INT. NIMUE'S CORNER. AVALON ABBEY. DAY.</u>

MERLIN is sitting on one side of the screen, lit by candles. In the dark, on the other side of the screen, there is a woman, NIMUE, dressed like a nun. Her face is veiled.

White butterflies dance around her, their wings catching the sunlight.

                         MERLIN:
          Nimue …

                         NIMUE:
          Merlin …

Their voices tremble in the air, like the butterflies.

                         MERLIN:
          How are you, my love?

NIMUE's hand suddenly appears at the grille. It is scarred and twisted. It is a terrible shock to us … But not to MERLIN.

He kneels and tenderly touches NIMUE's hand.

                         MERLIN:
          Nimue, Nimue, you are my sunlight … without you I'm lost …

                         OLD MERLIN'S VOICE:
          I was young and so much in love then …

NIMUE withdraws her hand and changes the subject.

                         NIMUE:
          Tell me about Arthur.

MERLIN:
He's golden … fine, handsome … everything I dreamed he'd be . . .

7.   EXT. FOREST. DAY.

Horses' hooves galloping through the forest.

The exultant figure of ARTHUR, young and handsome charges past.

OLD MERLIN'S VOICE:
(sadly)
It's true, then he was all those things … there was a glory about him …

8.   EXT. MERLIN'S COTTAGE. FOREST. DAY.

The cottage stands in an idyllic setting. It used to be AMBROSIA's old home but now the forest has reclaimed most of the building. The circular clearing is littered with ANIMALS and piles of branches and leaves which gives it a magical sense of nature. Everywhere we notice things laid out in circles. There are circles drawn on the cottage walls and a small circular table, made out of a tree trunk.

MERLIN sits on a log, trying hard to persuade a WHITE BUTTERFLY to co-operate.

MERLIN:
Avalon Abbey really isn't very far …

The BUTTERFLY hovers next to MERLIN's right ear as if whispering to him.

MERLIN:
What? … Speak up … Ah … I know you only live for a few days … it won't take you that long and you'd be doing me a great favour …
(the BUTTERFLY bobs up and down)
Thank you so much …

The BUTTERFLY flutters away as ARTHUR charges into the clearing and leaps off his HORSE almost before it stops.

MERLIN: *
Arthur, don't charge around like that, the horses don't like it! Don't dismount … we're leaving immediately!

ARTHUR'S HORSE neighs in agreement but ARTHUR is too impatient with important news to notice.

> ARTHUR:
> Merlin, have you heard the news? King Uther's dead.

MERLIN's only reaction is to whistle sharply and his horse, RUPERT comes trotting out from behind the house.

> ARTHUR:
> Didn't you hear what I said? ... The king's dead!

> MERLIN:
> I know.

He mounts his HORSE.

> ARTHUR:
> Know? Nobody got the news as fast as I did. How could you know out here in the woods?

> MERLIN:
> A little bird told me ...

A bewildered ARTHUR remounts.

> ARTHUR:
> Where are we going?

> MERLIN:
> To make you king.

9. <u>EXT. FOREST. DAY.</u>

BIRDS fly high over the TINY FIGURES of MERLIN and ARTHUR riding through the forest.

10. <u>EXT. FOREST. DAY.</u>

<u>CLOSE SHOT: MERLIN and ARTHUR.</u> As they ride through the forest ARTHUR is itching to ask questions but MERLIN glares at him every time he starts to open his mouth. At last, ARTHUR can stand it no longer and bursts out.

ARTHUR:
Tell me, how can I be king?!

MERLIN:
Because you were born to it.

ARTHUR:
(laughing)
I've no royal blood in me.

MERLIN:
Sir Hector isn't your real father.

ARTHUR stops laughing.

ARTHUR:
What?!

MERLIN:
Your father was King Uther. You're the true heir to the throne!

11.   EXT. FOREST. LATER THAT DAY. **

CLOSE SHOT: THREE GRIFFINS IN THE TREES. They have panther-like
bodies, exaggerated rib-cages, savage claws and their heads are covered with
hawk-hoods.

A WOMAN'S elegant hand comes INTO SHOT. A magnificent ruby ring on
her finger sparkles blood red as the hand removes the GRIFFINS' hoods to
reveal their heads and beaks. They spit and snarl.

Spreading their bat-wings, they launch themselves off their branches.

12.   EXT. FOREST. LATER THAT DAY. **

From the GRIFFINS' point-of-view, we see a STRANGELY DISTORTED
IMAGE OF MERLIN and ARTHUR below, riding through the forest between
grotesquely gnarled trees.

CLOSE SHOT: ARTHUR and MERLIN. There is a great screeching sound.
They look up to see a flurry of wings as the GRIFFINS attack. The FIRST
ONE knocks ARTHUR from his horse. As it goes in for the kill, ARTHUR
slashes at it with his sword, whilst MERLIN jumps down from his horse and
beats off the other TWO vicious GRIFFINS who are screeching like banshees.

A GRIFFIN'S claw tears at ARTHUR's arm as the OTHER GRIFFINS beat MERLIN to the ground.

CLOSE SHOT: MERLIN. He sees something in the tree above him.

CLOSE SHOT: WASPS' NEST. MERLIN sees a WASPS' nest.

CLOSE SHOT: MERLIN. He makes a small but distinctive gesture with his right hand.

CLOSE SHOT: WASPS'S NEST. Thanks to MERLIN, the WASPS come swarming out of their nest.

CAMERA BACK to show a CLOUD OF WASPS flying past ARTHUR and MERLIN and attacking the GRIFFINS by clustering round their eyes and stinging them repeatedly. The GRIFFINS let out unearthly howls and fly blindly away, smashing into the trees as they try to escape the fearsome WASPS.

TWO WASPS remain, hovering in the air above MERLIN as he gets up and nods to them.

                    MERLIN:
          Thank you ...

The TWO remaining WASPS dart away to join the OTHERS. ARTHUR staggers up.

                    ARTHUR:
               (answering MERLIN)
          I did nothing ...

                    MERLIN:
          I wasn't talking to you ...

A confused ARTHUR looks at MERLIN as he takes out a small container from his pocket and sprinkles powder over the wound.

                    ARTHUR:
          What was that?

                    MERLIN:
               (ironically)
          A calling card, from an old friend.

13.   <u>EXT. FOREST. DAY.</u> **

ARTHUR and MERLIN ride out of the wood onto a sunlit hillside.

                                        DISSOLVE TO:

14.   <u>EXT. RUINS BY A RIVER. NIGHT.</u> **

MERLIN and ARTHUR have made camp among some Roman ruins by a river.

They are crouched down beside a camp fire. ARTHUR is impatiently waiting for MERLIN to explain but MERLIN finds it difficult.

MERLIN'S HORSE, RUPERT, neighs impatiently and MERLIN gets up to tend him.

                    RUPERT:
        You're just putting it off, Merlin ... you have to tell him.

ARTHUR'S HORSE interjects.

                    ARTHUR'S HORSE:
        Tell him <u>everything</u>. I would if I were you.

                    RUPERT:
        Do you mind? This is a private conversation. No-one asked for your opinion!

                    MERLIN:
        No, no, it's good advice, from both of you. I just hope I know how to do it.

He moves back to join ARTHUR. We watch him over the HORSE'S HEADS.

                    ARTHUR'S HORSE:
        He's not bad for a human. Most of them are cruel, loud and vulgar.

<u>CLOSE SHOT: MERLIN and ARTHUR.</u> MERLIN sits beside ARTHUR in front of the camp fire.

                    ARTHUR:
                (impatiently)
        Are you going to tell me now?

MERLIN:
Yes … it's time.

As MERLIN settles down to talk, CAMERA BEGINS TO TRACK BACK and their VOICES FADE.

OLD MERLIN'S VOICE:
And so I began to tell him the story of my life, and times … bloody times … terrible times …

15.   EXT. PENDRAGON CASTLE. DUSK.

A fierce fireball from a great catapult hurtles across the black sky.

OLD MERLIN'S VOICE:
King Constant, Arthur's grandfather, was the first Christian king of England …

The fireball smashes on the battlements, illuminating the hard-pressed DEFENDERS and the REBEL ARMY below, laying siege to the castle.

OLD MERLIN'S VOICE:
King Constant was a good man who became a tyrant …

16.   INT. PASSAGEWAY. PENDRAGON CASTLE. DUSK. *

CLOSE SHOT: KING CONSTANT. A flaming torch in one hand and a bloodstained sword in the other, the Lear-like figure of CONSTANT, emerges out of the darkness, with unkempt long, white hair and clothes ripped.

CONSTANT:
Kill, kill, kill, kill all the prisoners! No mercy … no traitors … let the world die if I die!

17.   EXT. PENDRAGON CASTLE. DUSK.

The REBEL ARMY throw grappling ropes up to the battlements whilst their ARCHERS follow them up with storms of arrows. CONSTANT can be seen on the battlements, yelling and screaming.

18.   <u>INT. COURTYARD. PENDRAGON CASTLE. NIGHT.</u>

A battering-ram smashes through the great doors of the castle and the REBEL ARMY pours in and over the walls. CONSTANT is seized on the battlements and his MEN begin to surrender.

The noise of the fighting dies away. There is the sound of a HORSE approaching and the figure of VORTIGERN, in black armour and on a pure WHITE HORSE comes into the courtyard. He is a young man, big and powerful, in his prime. He rides towards the stairs.

His MEN drag the mad CONSTANT down from the battlements.

18A.   <u>INT. THRONE ROOM. PENDRAGON CASTLE. NIGHT.</u> *

VORTIGERN rides into the great hall.

CONSTANT is dragged into the hall still screaming defiance.

> CONSTANT:
> Traitors! … Die! Die! Die! … You'll all die! … My son, Uther, will avenge me! You'll never sleep easy, knowing he'll come for you, Vortigern!

> VORTIGERN:
> (softly)
> Where is he?

> CONSTANT:
> Safe in France!

As he laughs hysterically, OTHER REBEL SOLDIERS rush up.

> REBEL CAPTAIN:
> Prince Vortigern, he's had all the prisoners slaughtered.

There is a roar of hatred from the REBEL ARMY. "Justice! Justice!" The furious REBELS look up at VORTIGERN, who pauses, then reluctantly nods his head, the REBELS cheer and drag CONSTANT away screaming to the other end of the hall. VORTIGERN dismounts and moves to the throne. *

> CONSTANT:
> I curse you all!

19.   <u>INT. THRONE ROOM. PENDRAGON CASTLE. NIGHT.</u> *

<u>CLOSE SHOT: SHADOW ON A WHITE WALL.</u> It is the shadow of
CONSTANT being forced to his knees and his crowned head bowed. The
shadow of a sword flashes down and his head is lopped off and his shadow
crown rolls away.

20.   INT. THRONE-ROOM. PENDRAGON CASTLE. NIGHT.

The real crown of Britain rolls across the floor to VORTIGERN's feet. He
bends down, picks it up and puts it on his head. His MEN, crowding round,
raise their swords and proclaim him king.

21.   EXT. PATH. COUNTRYSIDE. DAY.

A band of bloodstained KNIGHTS thunder past.

                    OLD MERLIN'S VOICE:
          That was just the beginning … Civil war tore the country apart.

22.   EXT. VILLAGE. DAY

A vicious fight takes place in a small village with SOLDIERS and KNIGHTS
with swords and axes, hacking each other to pieces, ignoring the cries of
women and children.

23.   SCENE OMITTED.

24.   INT. CHURCH. DAY.

THREE PRIESTS kneel in prayer in front of the altar.

                    OLD MERLIN'S VOICE:
          Then the Saxons came …

The church door bursts open and SAXON WARRIORS rush in with black
metal helmets that half cover their faces and wielding battleaxes.

A SAXON WARRIOR flings an axe into the back of a PRIEST. The OTHERS
are butchered where they pray.

                    OLD MERLIN'S VOICE:
          Christian churches were destroyed and defiled … so were the
          sacred places of the old pagan religion …

25.   EXT. SACRED STONES. DUSK.

GUDRUN, a dying HIGH PRIESTESS of the Old Ways, crawls in front of the
altar stone and props herself up against another broken stone. *

GUDRUN: *
Mab! … Queen Mab! … Queen Mab! …

A FIGURE forms out of the great rock - it is QUEEN MAB. She is a darkly
beautiful woman. Powerful and charismatic, she is dressed sleekly in glittering
robes and has the ruby ring on her finger which we have seen before with the
GRIFFINS. *

GUDRUN: *
Ah, Lady … why didn't you come before? … I've followed you
all my life and now it's ending. We are in Hell! ... you must
stop the killings?

QUEEN MAB comes down and crouches beside her. *

MAB: *
I no longer have the power, Gudrun … too many of my
followers have foresaken the Old Ways and become Christian.

GUDRUN: *
(fiercely)
Fight! ... come out of the land of magic and fight for what we
once had ... then the people will come back to the Old Ways as if
new-born ... fight, Lady!

She holds out a bloodstained hand. QUEEN MAB takes it. *

MAB: *
I swear to bring back the Old Ways!

GUDRUN: *
Raise me up ... I want to see the sun go down for the last time,
before I die.

MAB helps GUDRUN stand upright, painfully, and the TWO WOMEN watch
the sun sink below the horizon and DARKNESS descend.

26.   EXT. LAKE. DAWN.

MAB walks pensively along the edge of the lake. It is a beautiful morning.
MAB stops, deep in thought.

The calm surface of the lake begins to ripple and bubble. Suddenly, magically, waves appear though there is no wind, the surface of the lake is whipped up by a storm. Waves crash, a water spout gushes high into the air.

Then they suddenly stop as if on command and the lake immediately becomes calm again. Something white flashes under the surface and the beautiful fair-haired LADY OF THE LAKE rises out of the water and floats across to the shore where MAB is waiting for her. She looks and acts as if still underwater. She has a neck lace of live fish.

> LADY OF THE LAKE:
I got your message, sister.

> MAB:
I've come to a great decision.

> LADY OF THE LAKE:
Oh … I don't like the sound of your voice when you say that, sister.

> MAB:
I'm going to create a leader for the people … a powerful wizard who'll save Britain and bring the people back to us and the Old Ways.

> LADY OF THE LAKE:
It'll be too much for you, Mab. It'll drain you of what power you still have.

> MAB:
If I don't do it we'll die … if people stop believing in us we won't exist … The new religion has already pushed us to the margin, soon we'll be forgotten.

> LADY OF THE LAKE:
All things change, sister … it's sad but heaven, hell and the world move on … it's Fate.

> MAB:
I won't accept it! I'll fight! Will you help me?

> LADY OF THE LAKE:
No … you forget I'm the Lady of the Lake … I'm made of water … now everything's flowing away from us and I accept it … I'm sorry, my dear.

CLOSE SHOT: MAB. She remains grimly determined.

                    MAB:
            Then I'll do it myself!

27.   INT. MAB'S CAVE. ENCHANTED LAND. DAY.

MAB's cave is furnished like a study but has hundreds of coloured crystals instead of books. They dazzle the eye with their vivid colours of the rainbow. They seem to pulse with energy.

MAB stares into a cluster of large crystals on the table as her Jeeves-like manservant, FRIK, a bony gnome, dressed in traditional striped morning suit and tails.

                    MAB:
            You heard that, Frik?

                    FRIK:
            I'm afraid your sister is rather indecisive when it comes to
            making decisions, Madam. She never gives you the backing
            you deserve.

                    MAB:
            We're on our own. I'd better get started.

                    FRIK:
            Don't you think you should at least wait a few days? ... to build
            up your strength.

                    MAB:
            There's no time, our world is dying.

FRIK nods and takes a step backwards as MAB "freezes" and concentrates all her powers on the crystals.

CLOSE SHOT: CRYSTALS. In each crystal there appears dozens of moving images of MERLIN.

CAMERA BACK to show MAB and FRIK looking at the images in the crystals. MAB is enchanted.

                    MAB:
            He's magnificent! ... Now, I have to give him life.

She concentrates even harder, silently summoning all her magic powers. There is a moment's silence, then without warning, ALL the crystals implode. A plume of coloured smoke rises from the crystals, draining them of their colour until they are clear.

28.   EXT. AMBROSIA'S COTTAGE. FOREST. DAWN.

There is a loud, lusty cry of a new-born BABY from inside the small cottage.

29.   INT. AMBROSIA'S COTTAGE. DAWN.

AMBROSIA, a short, feisty, middle-aged woman, wraps the new-born CHILD in a blanket and shows it to the mother, ELISSA, who lays on the bed, sweating and in terrible pain.

                         AMBROSIA:
          It's a beautiful boy.

ELISSA looks at lovingly, holds the BABY for a moment then painfully gives it back to AMBROSIA.

                         ELISSA:
          I'm dying …

                         AMBROSIA:
          No, no …

                         ELISSA:
          You've done so much for me … taken me in when they all
          shunned me … Now I ask you to do something more …
          please…
                    (she tugs desperately at AMBROSIA)
          Look after my baby, I beg you, I beg you! …

AMBROSIA attempts to calm her.

                         ELISSA:
                    (fiercely)
          Swear it!

                         AMBROSIA:
          I swear …

ELISSA becomes calm

AMBROSIA:
Good … now sleep … I'll take care of the child …

She turns away from the bed to find QUEEN MAB standing in front of her.
FRIK hovers discreetly in the background.

MAB:
Let me see the child!

AMBROSIA hands her the BABY. QUEEN MAB looks at it for a moment,
then smiles and holds it up in triumph.

MAB:
I name this child Merlin!

AMBROSIA:
(sharply)
Well, while you're making gestures, save the mother, she's
dying.

MAB:
No, she isn't, she's dead.

AMBROSIA turns back to the bed to find ELISSA is indeed dead. AMBROSIA
shakes her head sadly and gently pulls the bed blanket over her face.

AMBROSIA:
Sleep easy, child, may angels fly thee home …

She suddenly turns fiercely on QUEEN MAB.

AMBROSIA:
What's the excuse! Why didn't you save her?!

MAB:
She'd served her purpose!

AMBROSIA:
Served her purpose? Served her purpose?! You're so cold, if I
punched you in the heart I'd break my fist! … And to think I
once served you in the Old Ways.

MAB:
Then you changed and became a Christian.

AMBROSIA:
Who told you that?
                    (she points to FRIK)
That snooping, smiling blather-skite! … I'm not a Pagan or
Christian. I've tried 'em both and they've both failed me. I
follow my own heart, that's religion enough for me.

FRIK:
Why do you allow her to talk to you like that, Madam?

AMBROSIA:
Because she needs me, idiot! I'm sure you're called a big thinker
by people who lisp.

MAB:
Why do I need you, Ambrosia?

AMBROSIA takes the BABY from her.

AMBROSIA:
To take care of this child.

MAB:
I can take care of him!

A FAIRY flies in with a twig in its hand. Suddenly the hut is filled with
FAIRIES, ALL carrying twigs and feathers, and they begin to build a crib.

Then a swarm of BEES fly in and build a honeycomb on an empty plate.

Through the doorway an ELF is seen milking a goat. Fairies fly in a jug of milk
beside the newly-built crib.

The FAIRIES and BEES disappear as suddenly as they came, leaving the hut
spick and span but AMBROSIA distinctly unimpressed.

AMBROSIA:
Tricks! … You need more than tricks to bring up a child, you
don't know the first thing about it, do you? … you need
patience, understanding and love … above all you need LOVE
… that's something you had once but no more.

MAB scowls and FRIK winces, fearful at what her reaction is going to be. But
MAB's mood changes abruptly.

MAB:
You always had a viper's tongue, Sister Ambrosia, but you always spoke the truth as you saw it ...
(she glares at FRIK)
It's a commodity in very short supply in my court.

AMBROSIA:
So, what've you decided?

MAB:
The boy stays with you ... Remember he's only half human and he belongs to me ... he's my son! I'll send for him when it's time.

She vanishes. FRIK lingers.

AMBROSIA:
I don't know what I'll do without you, but I'd rather! ... GO!

FRIK hastily vanishes. AMBROSIA spots a FAIRY that has curled up asleep in a corner. She quietly opens the front door and boots the FAIRY out.

AMBROSIA:
And stay out!

AMBROSIA puts the BABY gently into the new crib.

OLD MERLIN'S VOICE:
Ambrosia was like a tiger protecting me. She was the bravest, kindest person I ever knew ... I called her Auntie A but she was really a mother to me ... It's strange I had no father but three mothers, my natural mother, my adopted mother and Queen Mab...

30.   SCENE OMITTED.

31.   INT. AMBROSIA'S COTTAGE. DAY.

With her sleeves rolled up and her face red from the steam from the cooking pots, AMBROSIA puts some hot dishes on the table, already groaning with food.

Like any normal boy, YOUNG MERLIN, now 17 years old, rushes in to sit down at the table, but AMBROSIA points to the sink.

AMBROSIA:
Wash your hands, Merlin … You've been talking with those red squirrels again.

YOUNG MERLIN washes his hands in a basin of water.

AMBROSIA:
That's a good boy … and your hair needs a good wash too … after you've eaten.

YOUNG MERLIN:
What've we got, Auntie A?

AMBROSIA:
One of your favourite's, dear - buttered parsnips.

YOUNG MERLIN licks his lips in anticipation as he quickly dries his hands and rushes across to the dinner table to tuck into a plate of buttered parsnips. AMBROSIA looks on with pride and love as he eats greedily.

31A.   INSERT.

CLOSE SHOT: OLD MERLIN. He licks his lips at the thought of those buttered parsnips.

OLD MERLIN: *
Ah, those buttered parsnips ... I can still taste Auntie Ambrosia's buttered parsnips ... That was the day everything changed forever.

32.   EXT. FOREST. DAY.

CLOSE SHOT: YOUNG MERLIN. He lays asleep by the side of the forest path. He opens his eyes and blinks.

CAMERA BACK to show he is looking up at YOUNG NIMUE, a beautiful sixteen-year-old girl. The sun is directly behind her and for a moment it looks as thought she has a golden halo.

She has several MALE and FEMALE SERVANTS who have to walk their HORSES through the forest as the path is overgrown. They laugh as YOUNG MERLIN staggers sleepily to his feet, nearly lurching into YOUNG NIMUE.

YOUNG NIMUE:
Please excuse their rudeness ... we're travelling to Lord
Lambert's castle and we've lost our way.

YOUNG MERLIN points.

YOUNG MERLIN: *
It's about a mile ... take the right fork but don't try any short
cuts, its dangerous and you can get lost.

YOUNG NIMUE:
Thank you, sir ... what can we offer you as a reward?

YOUNG MERLIN, who is not used to dealing with people, is bold.

YOUNG MERLIN:
A kiss.

There are shocked gasps from the FEMALE SERVANTS.

FIRST FEMALE SERVANT:
Do you know who you're talking to?

SECOND FEMALE SERVANT:
This is Lady Nimue.

YOUNG MERLIN:
Who?

SECOND FEMALE SERVANT:
(shocked)
Lord Ardent's daughter!

YOUNG MERLIN:
She asked me what I wanted and I told the truth.

YOUNG NIMUE:
(laughing)
And I think it's a fair price ...

She offers him her hand. YOUNG MERLIN takes it, kisses it, then looks into
YOUNG NIMUE's eyes. He pulls her to him and kisses her. It is a magic
moment for both of them.

YOUNG MERLIN:
My name's Merlin.

> YOUNG NIMUE:
> Mine's Nimue ...
> (she recovers)
> And you're a very rude young man!

> YOUNG MERLIN:
> I'll never forget you, Nimue ... We'll meet again ... I can see it!

For a moment YOUNG NIMUE believes him, then the moment is over.

> YOUNG NIMUE:
> I don't think so, Master Merlin.

She turns quickly and joins her SERVANTS and they move off down the path through the forest, the WOMEN giggling and laughing.

YOUNG NIMUE takes one furtive glance over her shoulder at YOUNG MERLIN before vanishing into the forest.

YOUNG MERLIN lays back on the ground and sighs, thinking of the young girl he has just met.

As NIMUE and her servants walk on through the forest they come up to *
the fork in the path and take the right one but find it is blocked by branches. Servants shout and point to a way round the barrier and they take it.

> DISSOLVE TO:

33.   EXT. FOREST. LATER THAT DAY.

YOUNG MERLIN, who has been laying on the ground, dreaming, suddenly sits bolt upright as he hears and "sees" something.

> OLD MERLIN'S VOICE:
> I could suddenly hear someone calling for help ... I knew it was Nimue ... and then I "saw" her ...

33A.   EXT. FOREST. DAY.

YOUNG MERLIN runs desperately through the forest.

33B.   <u>EXT. MUD HOLE. FOREST. DAY.</u>

YOUNG NIMUE has fallen into a treacherous mud hole which is sucking her down like quicksands. The more she struggles, the deeper she sinks. She has already sunk up to her armpits.

As she screams in fear, YOUNG MERLIN rushes into the clearing.

YOUNG NIMUE:
Help me! ... Help me!

YOUNG MERLIN:
I'm here! ... Don't struggle, you'll only sink deeper ... Stay
calm ...

He comes to the edge of the mud hole to reach out to her, but she is too far
away. He looks around, sees a broken branch and tries to get YOUNG
NIMUE to grab it, but it is too short.

As YOUNG NIMUE continues sinking, she cries out in fear ...

ACT ONE BREAK

YOUNG NIMUE continues sinking into the mud hole as YOUNG MERLIN
tries to reach her with a branch ...

OLD MERLIN'S VOICE:
That's when it happened...

33C.   INSERT

CLOSE SHOT: OLD MERLIN. He looks transfixed as he remembers.

OLD MERLIN:
I felt the power in me ... after all these years I still remember
how it was ...

33D.   EXT. MUD HOLE. FOREST. DAY.

CLOSE SHOT: YOUNG MERLIN. A desperate YOUNG MERLIN mutters
fiercely at the BRANCH in his hand.

YOUNG MERLIN:

Grow ... Grow ... Grow now!

The BRANCH magically grows longer.

CAMERA BACK to show YOUNG MERLIN holding the branch over the mud hole for YOUNG NIMUE. Now it is twice as long and she grabs it easily.

With newly acquired strength, YOUNG MERLIN pulls YOUNG NIMUE out of the treacherous mud and onto the bank.

The TWO flop down, exhausted.

> YOUNG MERLIN:
> I told you we'd meet again.

> YOUNG NIMUE:
> How did you do that ... with the branch?

> YOUNG MERLIN:
> I don't know.

> YOUNG NIMUE:
> Whatever it was, you saved my life. You deserve one more kiss for that.

She kisses him.

> YOUNG MERLIN:
> Only one?

YOUNG NIMUE kisses him again and they both find themselves so covered with mud, they burst out laughing.

34.   INT. AMBROSIA'S COTTAGE. DAY.

AMBROSIA is bustling about cleaning the cottage when YOUNG MERLIN rushes in, dripping wet and bursting with news.

> YOUNG MERLIN:
> I've seen her! ... the most beautiful girl in the world ... the only girl I'll ever love ... I know it ... and she loves me ... and we'll love each other always! ...

> AMBROSIA:
> (laughing)
> What're you babbling about? ... and you're dripping wet ... take off your clothes!!

YOUNG MERLIN pulls off his jerkin and she gets a towel to vigorously dries him.

YOUNG MERLIN:
I'm a hero too, I saved her …

AMBROSIA:
Saved who? … from what?

YOUNG MERLIN:
Nimue … Nimue … Nimue … she's the daughter of some lord … she fell into a mud hole and I saved her …

AMBROSIA:
(smiling)
Very brave of you, dear.

YOUNG MERLIN:
The extraordinary thing was how I saved her … I had this branch … and somehow I made it grow...

AMBROSIA suddenly stops drying him, and she is no longer smiling.

YOUNG MERLIN:
I know it sounds impossible but I said "Grow! Grow!" and … it grew … What's the matter, Auntie A?

He sees AMBROSIA has turned pale and sways.

AMBROSIA:
Help me to a chair, my dear.

A frightened YOUNG MERLIN helps AMBROSIA into a chair.

YOUNG MERLIN:
Tell me what's the matter.

AMBROSIA:
It's the moment I've been dreading all these years … it's time for you to leave.

YOUNG MERLIN:
Leave? I don't understand.

AMBROSIA:
I found your mother wandering in the forest alone and close to
her time. I took her in when you were born. I raised you and
loved you.

YOUNG MERLIN:
I love you, Auntie A.

AMBROSIA:
You have no father. There's magic at work here. You were
created by Queen Mab. And now she wants you to join her.

YOUNG MERLIN:
I won't.

AMBROSIA:
You've no choice, my dear. You cannot fight it - not yet ...

A bright light floods through the cottage window and there is the neighing of a
HORSE.

YOUNG MERLIN opens a window and looks out.

35.   EXT. AMBROSIA'S COTTAGE. DAY.

A GOLDEN HORSE waits for YOUNG MERLIN in front of the cottage. It has
a golden mane and tail and white body. It paws the ground with its front
hooves.

36.   INT. AMBROSIA'S COTTAGE. DAY.

YOUNG MERLIN looks out of the window at the HORSE, whilst
AMBROSIA rouses herself and gets him a warm jacket.

YOUNG MERLIN:
He's talking to me ... he says I have to go with him ...

AMBROSIA tenderly puts the jacket on YOUNG MERLIN.

AMBROSIA:
This will keep you warm on cold nights ...

>   YOUNG MERLIN:
>   (tearfully)
> Auntie A …
>
>   AMBROSIA:
> Now, now, chin up … magic has no power over the human
> heart … and don't forget what I taught you, never stop fighting
> for what's right …

They embrace.

>   YOUNG MERLIN:
> I love you, Auntie A.
>
>   AMBROSIA:
>   (fiercely)
> And tell Her Royal High and Mighty Queen Mab, magic or no
> magic, if she hurts you in any way, I'll have her guts for garters!

She kisses him for the last time.

37.   EXT. AMBROSIA'S COTTAGE. DAY.

YOUNG MERLIN comes out of the cottage and mounts the GOLDEN
HORSE. AMBROSIA stand in the doorway, watching him.

He turns and waves goodbye. AMBROSIA puts on a brave face and smiles.

The GOLDEN HORSE canters quickly away.

CLOSE SHOT: AMBROSIA. Only after YOUNG MERLIN is out of sight does
AMBROSIA break down and cry.

38.   EXT. FOREST. DAY

As YOUNG MERLIN rides the GOLDEN HORSE through the forest, he is
aware that he is being watched and followed by ELVES and FAIRIES. The
ELVES scamper in and out of the trees on the ground, whilst the FAIRIES
whiz through the air on either side, through the branches, sometimes in focus,
sometimes out of focus.

39.   EXT. ENCHANTED LAKE. DAY.

YOUNG MERLIN and the GOLDEN HORSE come out of the forest onto the shore of a great lake. They stop at the water's edge beside a small boat.

YOUNG MERLIN dismounts.

YOUNG MERLIN:
Thank you … I suppose I'm to get in the boat?

The GOLDEN HORSE grunts agreement and YOUNG MERLIN steps into the boat which immediately begins to glide out into the lake.

DISSOLVE TO:

40.   EXT. ENCHANTED LAKE. LATER THAT DAY.

The boat glides silently across the flat, undisturbed water and disappears into the mist.

41.   EXT. ENTRANCE TO CAVE. ENCHANTED LAKE. DAY.

The boat and YOUNG MERLIN head for a cave in a huge rock which seems to have grown out of the lake.

42.   INT. CAVE. DAY.

The boat sails deep into the dark cave which turns into a long dark tunnel.

YOUNG MERLIN looks up to see FAIRIES, glowing like shooting stars, flash along the cavern ceiling.

There is a shout from out of the darkness further ahead. YOUNG MERLIN sees the figure of FRIK, maniacally running on the water towards him, whilst putting on a ship's captain's hat and jacket with splendid silver buttons. We see he now has a trim beard and moustache.

FRIK:
Sorry I'm late, the ship left without me … Coming aboard, sir.

He whips out a ship's whistle and pipes himself aboard. He immediately take up a position in the prow of the boat.

YOUNG MERLIN:
Who're you?

FRIK:
Shhh, I have to concentrate, there're treacherous waters, strong
current … unseen rocks … Arr Jim lad ...

A bemused YOUNG MERLIN sees a pole suddenly appear in FRIK's hands as
he stares down into the dark waters.

OLD MERLIN'S VOICE:
It was all so strange and new … and yet and yet … I had this
feeling I was coming home …

43.   INT. FAIRY KINGDOM. DAY.

The boat comes to a stop at the beginning of the fairy kingdom - a massive
catacomb which stretches high into the rock-face and as far as the eye can see.

YOUNG MERLIN gets off the boat and just stares, for the fairy kingdom is an
extraordinary place, full of ever-changing CREATURES, LIGHTS and
OBJECTS.

ROCKS grow to form outcrops, then vanish. CURTAINS OF LIGHT cause
jumps in scale and dimension. As FAIRIES and ELVES move through the
CURTAINS, their colours and features change. These CREATURES whiz
about at express speed. It's like the Manhattan mid-town tunnel in rush hour.

CRYSTALS of all shapes and sizes litter the whole kingdom. Some are in
enormous shells, split down the middle like a porthole set in the rock. There are
FIRES in some of the rock caves as FAIRIES fly STONES from one cave to
another. Some FAIRIES stagger, OTHERS can't even get lift-off as they are
carrying too much weight. There is even a GRIFFIN asleep in the crevice in a
rock.   *

As he leads YOUNG MERLIN through the kingdom, FRIK has changed from
a Sea Captain to a Japanese Tourist Guide with flag, cap and folded map. He
jerks the flag up and down.

FRIK:
Follow me, follow me … don't get lost, don't get lost!

FRIK guides YOUNG MERLIN up a steep flight of steps. There at the top
stands MAB, looking very regal, dressed in one of her finest gowns, complete
with a magnificent diadem, flashing with diamonds.

FRIK immediately turns himself into the faithful Jeeves-like butler we have seen before.

FRIK:
Your Majesty, may I present …

MAB cannot control her enthusiasm and takes YOUNG MERLIN's two hands and looks into his eyes.

MAB:
(softly)
Merlin … Merlin … You've come at last … Do you know who I am?

YOUNG MERLIN:
Queen Mab.

MAB:
Yes … I've waited so long … You've grown handsome and true … I did well when I created you …

She addresses the FAIRIES and ELVES.

MAB:
This is Merlin who comes to save us! He will bring the people back to the Old Ways!

ALL the CREATURES' cheers echo and re-echo throughout the kingdom. A dozen FAIRIES scatter out of caves like frightened birds.

44.   INT. MAB'S SANCTUM. DAY.

The sanctum is like a magnificent library room but instead of thousands of books on the shelves, there are thousands of CRYSTALS. Some are in water, others in cloth, others are being heated. There is a great pile of used and discarded CRYSTALS in one corner - broken and drained of colour.

MAB is in a throne-like chair, talking to YOUNG MERLIN with FRIK hovering in the background.

YOUNG MERLIN:
Why did you say you created me … my mother did.

MAB:
I gave you life ... So in a way you have two mothers.

YOUNG MERLIN:
Three ... Auntie A...

Merlin picks up an amber CRYSTAL and studies it.

YOUNG MERLIN:
Why am I here?

MAB:
To learn ... I'll teach you to become the most powerful wizard the world has ever known.

YOUNG MERLIN:
Why?

MAB:
To lead mortals back to us ... to the Old Ways.

YOUNG MERLIN:
What if I don't want to be a wizard?

MAB:
It's your destiny. Remember that branch and how you made it grow?

YOUNG MERLIN:
I don't know how I did it.

MAB:
That's why you're here - to learn ... Oh Merlin, Merlin, you'll soon know the power that's in you ... and once it's unleashed, you'll hold this world in the hollow of your hand!

She holds up her hand and Merlin likewise raises his unwittingly. She clenches her fist. Merlin can't prevent his own clenching over the crystal which crushes to dust in his hand.

45.   INT. CLASSROOM. MAB'S SANCTUM. DAY.

YOUNG MERLIN is taking his first lesson in a traditional classroom with a desk, rolls of ancient parchments, massive dusty books, astrological charts hanging on the walls and a blackboard covered with mystical symbols.

YOUNG MERLIN and FRIK, now looking like a pedantic schoolmaster in a gown, horn-rimmed spectacles and carrying a cane, listen to MAB lecturing whilst ELVES and FAIRIES peer in through the windows. MAB points to the books and charts.

>   MAB:
>   All the magic of the universe and all the spells you'll ever need
>   are in these books, Merlin.

>   YOUNG MERLIN:
>   I'll need a lifetime to read all those.

>   MAB:
>   You'll have a very long life.

>   YOUNG MERLIN:
>   If I'm half mortal, will I die?

>   MAB:
>   In the fullness of time. We can't change that. But we can change
>   form …

She reaches across to FRIK and grabs his hair, pulling the skin from his face to reveal an elegant, young FOP who smiles superciliously and has rose stuck behind his ear.

>   MAB:
>   But it is only an illusion … particularly in his case.

FRIK turns back into his SCHOOLMASTER personae.

>   MAB:
>   We can hurt, but we can't kill outright … only humans can do
>   that and they need no help from us. Sometimes we can see into
>   the future...

MAB stares and the mature MERLIN appears opposite YOUNG MERLIN.

>   MAB:
>   This is you as you will be.
>   YOUNG MERLIN:
>   Will I grow that old?

>   MERLIN:
>   Have a care, Young Merlin!

YOUNG MERLIN:

Sorry, sir.

MERLIN:

But you're right, try and stay as young inside as you are now.
People who grow old lack hope, they've been fooled too many
times and think life, on the whole, is a bad business ... That's
another thing you should watch, Young Merlin - don't start
giving advice.

He vanishes.

YOUNG MERLIN:

When I see visions will they come true?

MAB:

Perhaps ... but you have to develop your power, dear boy ...
Frik, it's your turn.

FRIK adjusts his glasses, pulls at his gown.

FRIK:

Master Merlin, there are three classes of magic, three stages of
progression to full wizard status. The first and lowest stage is
wizard by incantation - those who invoke spells by incantation -
"Abra-cadabra dev and chort" ...

A flower appears in a globlet.

FRIK:

The second stage wizards are hand-wizards whose magic is
performed by gestures of the hands and fingers ...

FRIK gestures and the flower withers and dies.

FRIK:

The third and highest stage of wizardry, the supreme exponents
of the magic arts, are wizards of pure thought who need no
words or gestures but by their will alone pierce the heavens.

Mab picks up the globlet and throws the water towards FRIK. The water
droplets freeze in mid-air just in front of FRIK's face.

FRIK:

Of course, only the most supremely gifted personages become
wizards of the third stage.

MAB:
Frik get on with it . . .

Mab snaps her fingers and we hear the offscreen sound of a splash. Cut to C/U FRIK, a wilted flower on his head and dripping wet.

46.   INT. CLASSROOM. MAB'S SANCTUM. NIGHT.

YOUNG MERLIN is studying ancient books propped up in front of him, illuminated by GLOWWORMS.

OLD MERLIN'S VOICE:
I studied day and night ... and learned of those unseen forces that hold this world together ... learnt the secret ways of other worlds that exist beneath the surface and behind the mirrors ...

47.   INT. CLASSROOM. MAB'S SANCTUM. DAY.

FRIK and YOUNG MERLIN sit opposite each other, looking at an unlit candle on the table in front of them.

FRIK gestures with his right hand and the CANDLE LIGHTS ITSELF. He gestures with his left hand and the CANDLE IS EXTINGUISHED.

FRIK:
Now you try.

YOUNG MERLIN is bored.

YOUNG MERLIN:
Must I?

FRIK:
(frustrated)
Yes! ... Right hand, sir, right hand! ...

YOUNG MERLIN gestures with his right hand and the CANDLE LIGHTS ITSELF.

FRIK:
Now put it out ... left hand, left hand ... you must concentrate.

YOUNG MERLIN gestures with his left hand and the CANDLE EXPLODES, showering FRIK with pieces of hot wax.

FRIK:
That happened because you weren't concentrating!

48.   INT. MAB'S SANCTUM. DAY.

MAB is looking into a crystal ball as FRIK comes in.

MAB:
Well, how's he doing?

FRIK:
You've read my report?

MAB:
Yes, yes, but I want your personal impressions.

FRIK:
He's got the ability … he could be the greatest.

MAB:
Ah! I knew it.

FRIK:
But he'll never be … he won't get past being a Hand Wizard …
he doesn't want to do it … in his heart he doesn't like magic

MAB:
Doesn't like it?!

FRIK:
I know it's shocking but that's the way it is.

MAB:
We've got to make him like it! … I've got work for him to do.

FRIK:
The truth is, he wants to go home!

49.   INT. INNER LAKE. DAY.

YOUNG MERLIN is deeply unhappy.

As he stares at the lake in his frustration, he sees another lake beneath the surface. It is as if he is looking down through a glass bottom boat. Crystals glitter in the "second lake" and then the LADY OF THE LAKE appears floating between them.

                    LADY OF THE LAKE:
Why did you call me, Merlin?

                    YOUNG MERLIN:
I didn't.

                    LADY OF THE LAKE:
                (smiling)
You did …

                    YOUNG MERLIN:
Who are you?

                    LADY OF THE LAKE: *
The Lady of the Lake … how are you getting on with my sister Mab? We two don't get on.

                    YOUNG MERLIN:
Why?

                    LADY OF THE LAKE:
I don't approve of what she's been doing … creating you and letting your mother die like that …

                    YOUNG MERLIN:
                (slowly)
She let my mother die?

                    LADY OF THE LAKE: *
Oh dear, I shouldn't've told you but it just slipped out.

                    YOUNG MERLIN: *
I want to go home!

                    LADY OF THE LAKE:
You should, your Auntie Ambrosia is very ill.

YOUNG MERLIN is appalled.

50.   INT. CLASSROOM. MAB'S SANCTUM. DAY.

MAB and FRIK come into the classroom. There is no sign of YOUNG
MERLIN.

                          FRIK:
                Where is he?

51.   EXT. ENCHANTED LAKE. DAY.

YOUNG MERLIN sails the boat home, through the mists.

52.   INT. CLASSROOM. MAB'S SANCTUM. DAY.

MAB turns in a fury to FRIK who has turned back into his BUTLER role.

                          MAB:
                He's on his way home to that viper-tongued witch, Ambrosia.

                          FRIK:
                How can he get across the lake?

                          MAB:
                My dear sister …

FRIK:
Oh … if I may say so, Madam, it really would help matters if you two could agree to …

MAB:
When I want your advice, Frik, I'll ask for it.

FRIK:
As you wish, Madam. But what're you going to do?

MAB:
I'm not going to lose him!

53.   INT. AMBROSIA'S COTTAGE. DAY.

AMBROSIA is looking ill as she slowly and painfully crosses to the hob to get some hot water.

MAB suddenly appears in the room.

MAB:
Where is he?

AMBROSIA:
Ah, here you are again, still a chip off the old glacier. Please don't bother to knock!

MAB:
Where's Merlin?

AMBROSIA:
(tartly)
So you've lost him, have you? I must say it's typical, over the last few years you've been sliding down the ladder of success so fast, you must be getting splinters in your backside.

MAB:
Don't provoke me, Ambrosia. I'm in no mood for your jibes.

AMBROSIA:
I'm anxious about the boy, too. You should've looked after him better.

MAB:
He'll be here, he's heard you're ill.

AMBROSIA:
Ai, ai, I've seen better days. But I'm not ill, I'm dying.

She sits in a chair, exhausted.

MAB:
When he comes, send him back.

AMBROSIA:
Can't you make him come back?

MAB:
It's better if you tell him his place is with me.

AMBROSIA:
No. I won't do that.

MAB:
You defy me?

AMBROSIA:
Of course I defy you. I've always defied you.

MAB:
Why? Why?

AMBROSIA:
It's my nature ... When my boy comes here, I won't say a
word. He'll do what's in his heart!

MAB finally loses her temper, opens her mouth and lets out a terrible silent roar
of rage. An instant storm whips up causing havok and knocking pots flying.
The fire in the stove rages. Some pots hit Ambrosia's shoulder. The storm dies.
The shock is so great, AMBROSIA slumps forward in the chair, clutching her
chest.

MAB:
You see what you made me do ... Ambrosia ... Ambrosia ...
What is it?
She crosses to AMBROSIA who looks up weakly and smiles.

AMBROSIA:
You tell me. You're the great Mistress of Magic ...

YOUNG MERLIN comes in and sees AMBROSIA's condition and rushes to
her.

YOUNG MERLIN:
Auntie A! ... Auntie A! ...

He bends over her, she touches his face tenderly.

AMBROSIA:
Dear boy, dear boy, you came back.

YOUNG MERLIN:
What's wrong?

AMBROSIA:
Nothing ... everything's as it should be ... Merlin, Merlin ...
remember ... only listen to your heart ...

She dies. YOUNG MERLIN cries out in anguish, picks her up and lays her out
on the sofa. He turns savagely on MAB.

YOUNG MERLIN:
You killed her!

MAB:
No, I didn't.

YOUNG MERLIN:
You killed her like you killed my real mother!

MAB:
No, I only let her die.

He raises his hand to strike MAB but an unseen force prevents him.

MAB:
You haven't the power to strike me.

YOUNG MERLIN:
Watch my power grow!

Their eyes lock in battle. YOUNG MERLIN forces his hand down until it
almost touches MAB's face. But the unseen force finally pushes it aside.

MAB:
That was very good, Merlin, I'm impressed.

YOUNG MERLIN:
I'll never forgive you!

MAB:
I'm sorry about your mother and Ambrosia but they were
casualties of war. I'm fighting to save my people from
extinction.

YOUNG MERLIN:
I don't care if you die and disappear.

MAB:
I will, unless I fight and win. That's why you were created.

YOUNG MERLIN:
I'll never help you!

MAB:
You will. I'll make you … But you're too upset to talk about this
now … later, after you've grieved.

She disappears and YOUNG MERLIN turns back to AMBROSIA.

54.   EXT. COTTAGE. FOREST. DAY.

YOUNG MERLIN stands over the grave of AMBROSIA which he has just
dug.

YOUNG MERLIN: *
I swear on Ambrosia's grave and the grave of my mother, I'll
only ever use my powers to defeat Queen Mab, … this I swear.

He cuts his thumb with a knife and sprinkles the blood over the grave. Bright
RED FLOWERS spring up where the spots land.

OLD MERLIN'S VOICE:
And thus I set my course … I knew Mab had heard me, but right
from the start she believed she could make me break my oath.
After all, part of her was in me … So she waited patiently in the
shadows, for the time when she could strike and make me see
the error of my ways …

ACT TWO BREAK

55.   EXT. COTTAGE. FOREST. DAY.

Years have passed, and the fully mature MERLIN stands by AMBROSIA's grave.

                    OLD MERLIN'S VOICE:
            She had to wait years but it didn't matter... Those years passed
            as if in seconds … and then she found a way of making me
            break my oath …

56.   EXT. VORTIGERN'S NEW CASTLE. DAY.

CLOSE SHOT: NIMUE. She has now grown into a stunningly beautiful woman.

CAMERA BACK to show she is with her father, LORD ARDENT, a fawning courtier at VORTIGERN's camp site.

VORTIGERN watches MASONS build a tower for his new castle. He has grown much older in the past few years and has fought many battles. His face is scarred and his left arm is stiff and lifeless. The uneasy ARCHITECT and an OLD SOOTHSAYER are with him as he joins LORD ARDENT and NIMUE.

                    VORTIGERN:
            It's a fine position for a new castle, don't you think, Lord
            Ardent?

As always LORD ARDENT agrees.

                    LORD ARDENT:
            It'll be impregnable, Your Majesty. No army could take it.

                    VORTIGERN:
            Not even Uther's?

                    LORD ARDENT:
            My Lord Uther's in Normandy, sire.

                    VORTIGERN:
            My spies tell me he's raising an army and getting ready to sail
            for England. He wants to kill me. I can't blame him, I killed his
            father, King Constant.

                    LORD ARDENT:
            King Constant was a tyrant.

VORTIGERN:

Not unlike myself.

LORD ARDENT gives a sickly smile.

LORD ARDENT:

Yes sire, no, sire, no …

VORTIGERN:

You don't sound very convincing, Ardent. What I'm interested in, in case we'd have to fight, whose side will you be on. Mine or his?

LORD ARDENT:
(indignantly)
I've always been loyal to Your Majesty!

VORTIGERN:

True, true … up till now. The trouble is, I don't trust anyone anymore. I want guarantees.

LORD ARDENT:

You have my word on it.

VORTIGERN:

Not enough … I'm keeping your daughter as surety.
(to GUARDS)

Guards!

LORD ARDENT:

This is outrageous, sire.

VORTIGERN:

I'm sorry …

NIMUE:
(defiantly)
My father will do what is right!

VORTIGERN:

I hope he will, he never has before. If your father stays loyal to me you'll be safe, if he betrays me, I will kill you.

NIMUE:

Father! …

She is taken away by the GUARDS. LORD ARDENT hovers, brooding.
VORTIGERN turns his attention to the ARCHITECT.

VORTIGERN:
How does it go? Are you making any progress?

ARCHITECT:
Fine, sire, fine ... the linnets on the west side need bolstering ...

Suddenly there is a loud rumble. The MASONS start yelling and jum from the
scaffolding as the tower begins to crumble. There is a roar and the stone
structure crashes down.

VORTIGERN:
Please tell me exactly what happened?

ARCHITECT:
I don't know, sire.

VORTIGERN:
Guards, take him away.

ARCHITECT:
It shouldn't've done that ... It's the linnets! ... I'm sure it's the
linnets!

The GUARDS grab the ARCHITECT who clutches his plans.

VORTIGERN:
And get me a different architect.

As the GUARDS drag him away, VORTIGERN turns to the frightened OLD
SOOTHSAYER.

VORTIGERN:
Why won't the tower stand?

OLD SOOTHSAYER:
I'm a Soothsayer, Your Majesty ... not an Architect.

VORTIGERN:
So tell me, why is it that every time I try to build this tower it
collapses?!

OLD SOOTHSAYER:
Ah well … yes indeed … hhmm … you think I should know that?

VORTIGERN grabs him by the throat.

VORTIGERN:
<u>Yes</u>!

OLD SOOTHSAYER:
(choking)
Ahhh … I'll … I'll read the stones … I will ... that's something I do well ...

VORTIGERN releases him.

VORTIGERN:
Then read them!

VORTIGERN looks to heaven in frustration.

VORTIGERN:
Why? Why? Why am I surrounded by incompetant fools?

57.   EXT. SACRED STONES. NIGHT.

The OLD SOOTHSAYER crouches in front of a fire in the centre of the great circle of stones. He casts runes and sighs in despair.

OLD SOOTHSAYER:
I've been a worshipper of the Old Ways all my life … now that life is in danger … And it's a precious life - it's mine … I've never had any real help … no, never … what am I going to do? … I don't know why his tower keeps falling down …

MAB forms out of a stone.

MAB:
The land is cursed …

The OLD SOOTHSAYER gives a yell of fright.

OLD SOOTHSAYER:
You've appeared ... you've appeared after all these years ... It is
Queen Mab?

MAB:
Yes, old man ... the land is cursed. Neither the tower or castle
will stand.

OLD SOOTHSAYER:
So ... what do we do?

MAB:
You must find a man who has no mortal father and mix his
blood with the mortar.

OLD SOOTHSAYER:
Ooo, ahh, splendid ... but a man who has no mortal father? ...
Er, where can I find a man like that?

MAB:
I'll show you.

58.   EXT. AMBROSIA'S COTTAGE. DAY. **

MERLIN is waiting when a TROOP of VORTIGERN'S SOLDIERS ride up
with the OLD SOOTHSAYER.

OLD SOOTHSAYER: *
(blustering)
Seize that man!

MERLIN: *
(mildly)
Welcome to my home, sir. How can I help you?

The OLD SOOTHSAYER immediately changes his approach as he dismounts.

OLD SOOTHSAYER: *
Well, er, the king wants to see you.

MERLIN: *
You only have to ask.

OLD SOOTHSAYER: *
You'll come voluntarily? Ah, that's good, most people are reluctant to meet King Vortigern. In fact they're usually dragged in screaming - not that I blame them ... I'm the King's Soothsayer.

MERLIN: *
(ironically)
An important position?

OLD SOOTHSAYER: *
(sighing)
And a fragile one ... I'm the third Royal Soothsayer this year.

MERLIN: *
King Vortigern gets through them at an alarming speed?

OLD SOOTHSAYER: *
(shuddering)
He gets through everything at an alarming speed ... you're Merlin, a man without a mortal father?

MERLIN: *
Yes.

OLD SOOTHSAYER: *
I'm afraid the king wants you urgently.

59.   EXT. FOREST. DAY **

MERLIN and the OLD SOOTHSAYER ride slowly through the forest.

MERLIN: *
How did you find me?

OLD SOOTHSAYER: *
I am a professional Soothsayer.

MERLIN: *
Oh, yes, of course ... its obvious ...

60.   EXT. VORTIGERN'S NEW CASTLE. DAY.

VORTIGERN watches MASONS rebuilding the tower with a NEW
ARCHITECT who is visibly trembling as he clutches the building plans.

> NEW ARCHITECT:
> It'll hold this time, Your Majesty, never fear.

> VORTIGERN:
> I never have.

> NEW ARCHITECT:
> Good, good, the foundations are as solid as …

There is another loud crash as the MASONS jump clear of the scaffolding and
the tower collapses yet again.

Clouds of dust rise from the spot as VORTIGERN turns on the NEW
ARCHITECT with deadly calm.

> VORTIGERN:
> You were saying the foundations were as solid as … what was
> the word? … jelly!

Fortunately for the NEW ARCHITECT, just as VORTIGERN pulls out his
dagger, the OLD SOOTHSAYER canters up with MERLIN and the
SOLDIERS.

They dismount and MERLIN has to help the OLD SOOTHSAYER off his
horse.

> OLD SOOTHSAYER:
> Thank you, my boy … Your Majesty, I've found him - the man
> without a mortal father.

VORTIGERN puts the dagger to the OLD SOOTHSAYER's throat.

> VORTIGERN:
> If this is another of your moth-eaten tricks! …

> OLD SOOTHSAYER:
> No, no … it's all true.

> VORTIGERN:
> There's only one way to find out …

He suddenly turns and punches MERLIN to the ground before he can defend himself.

> VORTIGERN:
> Get the knife and bowl and cut his throat ...

The SOLDIERS look less than happy as they move towards MERLIN with a knife and bowl.

> VORTIGERN:
> I mean now, not next Tuesday! What's the matter with you?

> OLD SOOTHSAYER:
> He's a wizard.

> VORTIGERN:
> He doesn't look much of a wizard.

MERLIN recovers from the blow.

> MERLIN:
> You caught me by surprise, why do you want to cut my throat?

> VORTIGERN:
> It's not personal ... I have to mix your blood with the mortar in the castle. This toothless old fool says it's the only way to make the building stand. You'll die easier knowing you die for your country.

> MERLIN:
> I'm afraid, your Majesty is giving the impression of being invincibly stupid.

> VORTIGERN:
> What was that last word?

> MERLIN:
> Stupid.

There is a terrible pause. Then, unexpectedly, VORTIGERN roars with laughter.

> VORTIGERN:
> This man thinks he's me!

The OTHERS join in the laughter.

> VORTIGERN:
> Why did you call me stupid?

> MERLIN:
> Because it's obvious why you can't build a castle there …
> Look …

He points to two great rocks just below the base of the castle.

> VORTIGERN:
> I'm looking!

> NEW ARCHITECT:
> I don't see anything.

Then SOMETHING sparkles between the rocks.

> MERLIN:
> Can't you see the stream?! It runs into a great cavern below.

EVERYONE looks. There is a glint of water from a tiny STREAM.

VORTIGERN is stunned as the NEW ARCHITECT babbles.

> NEW ARCHITECT:
> There's no water there - I swear.

> OLD SOOTHSAYER:
> I can see it. We can all see it.

> VORTIGERN:
> You wanted to build a castle on water?!

> NEW ARCHITECT:
> But, but, but, but …

                              MERLIN:
                 That's not all that's wrong … you've woken the dragons.

                              VORTIGERN:
                 Dragons? What dragons? … What do you see?

MERLIN stares and goes into a TRANCE.

                              MERLIN:
                 I see two dragons … one red … one white …

                              VORTIGERN:
                 My crest has a white dragon.

                              DISSOLVE TO:

61.   INSERT: MERLIN'S VISION. TWO HUGE BANNERS appear on the mound
       in front of the castle. ONE has a GIANT RED DRAGON on it, the other a
       WHITE DRAGON.

       A wind swirls frantically about, making them whip against each other as if they
       were doing battle.

       The WHITE DRAGON seems to be stronger and dominates the RED for a time.
       But then the RED DRAGON banner gains in ferocity and the wind round the
       WHITE BANNER gradually stops blowing. The WHITE BANNER hangs
       limply on the pole.

                              DISSOLVE TO:

62.   EXT. VORTIGERN'S NEW CASTLE. DAY.

       MERLIN comes out of his TRANCE.

                              VORTIGERN:
                 What did you see?

                              MERLIN:
                 The red dragon conquered the white.

                              OLD SOOTHSAYER:
                 It's an omen … 'er, wouldn't you say sire? I mean it could be
                 an omen …

As VORTIGERN scowls at him, some KNIGHTS ride into the camp, including the lean SIR GILBERT and the perpetually twitchy SIR EGBERT. They dismount and hurry over to VORTIGERN.

> SIR EGBERT:
> Your Majesty, Prince Uther has landed from Normandy with a great army.

> SIR GILBERT:
> He's marching on Winchester.

VORTIGERN lets out a howl of rage, then suddenly remembers MERLIN, and looks at him with something like awe.

> VORTIGERN:
> You foresaw all this …

> MERLIN:
> I am Merlin, I see things unknown.

> SIR GILBERT:
> What're your orders, sire?

> VORTIGERN:
> Gather my armies. We march on Winchester … Why doesn't it ever stop? I've been fighting my enemies for twenty years. I crush one and another takes his place.

> MERLIN:
> Perhaps you need me to foretell the future, then you could crush them all before they had a chance to cause trouble.

> VORTIGERN:
> Yes, that would be helpful, Merlin.

> MERLIN:
> Of course, then you couldn't cut my throat?

> VORTIGERN:
> No … You're obviously an extraordinary man. But I can't have extraordinary men running loose ...

Again, without warning, he springs on MERLIN and knocks him unconscious with the butt of his sword.

> VORTIGERN:
> You're just not quick enough, it's a mistake my enemies make too. I act before I think, so I act first! That's why I always have the advantage ... Mount up, we ride for Pendragon Castle ...
> (to OLD SOOTHSAYER)
> Not you, you're out of a job!

> OLD SOOTHSAYER:
> But sire ...

> VORTIGERN:
> Why so surprised? You must've known this would happen, you're an expert on the future.

He hurries away, roaring with laughter, leaving behind a depressed OLD SOOTHSAYER.

63. EXT. PENDRAGON CASTLE. DAY.

Flaming torches light the courtyard as VORTIGERN at the head of his TROOPS rides into Pendragon Castle.

64. EXT. WINDOW. COURTYARD. PENDRAGON CASTLE. DAY.

NIMUE looks down at the courtyard and at the return of VORTIGERN.

Something catches her eye.

65. EXT. COURTYARD. PENDRAGON CASTLE. DAY.

NIMUE sees the unconscious MERLIN slung over a horse with his hands tied.

66. EXT. WINDOW. COURTYARD. PENDRAGON CASTLE. DAY.

NIMUE stares hard. She thinks she recognises the face. Could it be the YOUNG MERLIN who rescued her all those years ago?

67. INT. DUNGEONS. PENDRAGAON CASTLE. DUSK.

GUARDS carry MERLIN down the dungeon steps. A JAILER opens a cell door and MERLIN is pushed inside.

As the JAILER locks the cell door, MAB suddenly appears behind him. She looks at the lock - it is encircled with a blue light and seems to seal itself.

ACT THREE BREAK

68.   INT. MERLIN'S CELL. PENDRAGON CASTLE. DAY

MERLIN regains consciousness, gets up and looks around. As he does so Frik appears in his butler-like incarnation.

MERLIN:
Hello, Frik. How're you?

FRIK:
Overworked and underpaid ... you're in serious trouble this time, Master Merlin. How did they ever make a vulgarian like, Vortigern, king? You mortals have no sense of the fitness of things ... I'm here with a message from Mab.

MERLIN:
Naturally.

FRIK:
She's going to punish you.

MERLIN:
She hates me.

FRIK:
No, but she's very disappointed you've been so reluctant to use your magic power.

MERLIN:
I swore an oath on Ambrosia's grave.

FRIK:
But why won't you use them Master Merlin?

MERLIN:
(savagely)
Because Mab wants me to!

FRIK:
You will, in the end, you're half human ... she's a terrible enemy Master Merlin, and a very poor employer. But enough of my problems ...

He vanishes leaving MERLIN in the dark.

DISSOLVE TO:

69.   SCENE OMITTED.

70.   INT. MERLIN'S CELL. PENDRAGON. CASTLE. DAY.

Trapped in his dark cell, away from sunlight, MERLIN is getting weaker as he lies on his bunk.

                        NIMUE'S VOICE:
            Merlin? …

He gets up and crosses to the small barred window. If he stretches up he can just reach it.

CLOSE SHOT: MERLIN and NIMUE. MERLIN can see NIMUE's face on the other side of the grill. It is very like the scene when they met in the abbey at Avalon. MERLIN instantly recognises her.

                        MERLIN:
            Nimue!

                        NIMUE:
            Merlin, it is you! You said we'd meet again ... I thought I
            recognised you last night when they brought you in … but then
            they said you were a wizard.

                        MERLIN:
            Yes, I am.

                        NIMUE:
            Not much of one. You can't even escape.

MERLIN smiles wryly.

                        MERLIN:
            I can but I won't.

                        NIMUE:
                     (astonished)
            Why not?

                        MERLIN:
            That's between me and Queen Mab.

NIMUE crosses herself quickly.

                    NIMUE:
She's leader of the Old Ways. We Christians hate her as an
enemy of the True Faith … are you a Christian?

                    MERLIN:
No, with me it's personal. Mab is my enemy because she
destroyed people I loved ... what're you doing here, Nimue?

                    NIMUE:
I'm a hostage. Vortigern wants to make sure my father doesn't
join Prince Uther.

                    MERLIN:
Why? ... Was he going to?

                    NIMUE:
No ... but Vortigern doesn't trust anyone even his few
remaining friends. Over the last few years he's got worse. It's
dangerous being near him, no-one knows who he'll strike down
next.

                    MERLIN:
It seems I said the wrong thing. I told him Uther would defeat
him.

                    NIMUE:
Oh, I pray you're right.

MERLIN stretches out his hand so their fingers touch. NIMUE smiles and presses her face closer to the grill. She sees how pale and sick MERLIN looks.

NIMUE:
What's the matter, Merlin, are you ill?

MERLIN:
I need space to breathe ... these four walls are suffocating me...
I've never forgotten you Nimue.

NIMUE:
I've always remembered you, Merlin.

OLD MERLIN'S VOICE:
And so the hours past ...

70A.   INT. MERLIN'S CELL. PENDRAGON CASTLE. NIGHT

Moonlight shines through the barred window as MERLIN lays on the bunk looking even weaker than before.

NIMUE appears at the window. MERLIN pulls himself off the bunk to go over to her.

OLD MERLIN'S VOICE:
Nimue came, day and night but it didn't help...

71.   INT. THRONE ROOM. PENDRAGON CASTLE. DAY.

VORTIGERN is in conference with his KNIGHTS, including the lean SIR GILBERT and the perpetually twitchy SIR EGBERT.

SIR GILBERT:
Uther's captured Winchester. He's unstoppable.

VORTIGERN slams his fist on the table.

VORTIGERN:
I'll stop him.

There is shouting from outside the throne room and NIMUE forces her way in, past the GUARDS.

VORTIGERN:
I didn't send for you!

NIMUE:
That's why I'm here.

VORTIGERN:
I've killed men for such insolence.

NIMUE:
And women?

VORTIGERN:
Yes, and children.

NIMUE:
(laughing)
See, I'm trembling!

VORTIGERN:
What makes you so brave?

NIMUE:
Knowing if you hurt me, my father and his men will go over to Uther.

VORTIGERN calms down. That's something he doesn't want.

VORTIGERN:
Yes, that would make you brave enough to face me … Now you're here, what do you want?

NIMUE:
Merlin the wizard is sick

VORTIGERN:
Get him a physician - I can't be expected to do everything.

NIMUE:
There's no cure but his freedom.

VORTIGERN:
No, I can't give him that.

NIMUE:
Then he'll die.

VORTIGERN:
Everybody dies … even wizards.

NIMUE:
If he does, you'll never know about the battle. He's had another vision, don't you want to know how to win?

72.   SCENE OMITTED

73.   INT. MERLIN'S CELL. PENDRAGON CASTLE. DAY.

MERLIN turns to see NIMUE come in. They move into each other's arms.

74.   EXT. COURTYARD. PENDRAGON CASTLE. DAY.

NIMUE and MERLIN walk across the sunlit courtyard to the throne room. He seems to drink in the bright sunshine.

MERLIN:
Why does Vortigern want to see me?

NIMUE:
Uther has taken Winchester ... Vortigern thinks if you tell him what you can see, he can change the future …

MERLIN looks up at the sun. NIMUE gently touches his face.

MERLIN takes her hand smiles quietly.

75.   INT. THRONE ROOM. PENDRAGON CASTLE. DAY.

VORTIGERN is with his KNIGHTS.

VORTIGERN:
I have the biggest army Britain has ever seen.

SIR EGBERT:
(nervously)
It may not be enough, Your Majesty. Uther and his men
follow the Christian way.

VORTIGERN:
I thought they didn't believe in killing?

SIR GILBERT:
They'll kill in a Holy Cause. And destroying you is a Holy
Cause.

VORTIGERN:
Very convenient ... they kill when it suits them.

SIR GILBERT:
Like all of us, sire.

VORTIGERN:
What I want to know is, when will he attack?

SIR EGBERT:
Not before Spring.

VORTIGERN:
If that's true I'll use Winter as my ally and take him by
surprise... if it's true.

MERLIN and NIMUE are ushered into the room.

VORTIGERN:
Ah, Merlin, I need your help ... I know I have been a little
hot tempered ... the cares of office ... patience was never
one of my virtues.

MERLIN:
You have so few, I wouldn't trouble myself about that one
too much sire ... what do you want?

VORTIGERN:
I have to know, can Uther be defeated?

MERLIN:
I dreamed a battle ... near Winchester ... but I couldn't see
how it ended, I was too weak.

VORTIGERN:
Dream it again! Now I've spared your life, it's the last we can
do ... I want to know who wins!

MERLIN:
And I want fresh air and sunlight! Without them I can't dream
dreams, see visions. I need the sun!

VORTIGERN:
Is that all? Why didn't you say so in the first place? There's
plenty of sun on the battlements and you can sniff up as much
free fresh air as you like.

76.   INT. NIMUE'S ROOM. PENDRAGON CASTLE. NIGHT.

MERLIN and NIMUE are sitting in NIMUE'S ROOM. The moon is shining
through the window.

NIMUE:
You really are a wizard?

MERLIN:
A Hand-Wizard.

NIMUE:
You mean there's magic in hands?

MERLIN:
They can say so much more than words ... a clenched fist,
snapping fingers, thumb up, thumb down, hands welcoming,
begging or praying... they're a universal language... hands
can even pluck down the moon for you ...

He stretches out and seems to pluck the moon out of the night sky and hold it
in his hand.

MERLIN:
If only we could keep everything simple, like the roundness of
the moon ... look at its simplicity Nimue ... everything equal
... no part more important than the rest...

He runs the moon over his fingers like a coin. Closing his hand he offers the
moon to NIMUE. Light glows from Merlin's fist as NIMUE accepts the gift.

MERLIN:
Ah, but the moon's not so easy to catch and hold ...

He opens his fist. His hand is empty. NIMUE laughs.

NIMUE:
I thought you weren't going to do any magic.

MERLIN:
That wasn't magic, magic's real ... that was a trick.

NIMUE:
How did you do it?

MERLIN:
It's a secret ... and if I told you it wouldn't be a secret
anymore.

NIMUE:
Can you tell me something plain ... without tricks, Merlin?

MERLIN:
Yes ... just ask.

NIMUE:
What do you want?

MERLIN:
I want you.

NIMUE:
That's not what I meant ... what do you want from life?

> MERLIN:
> I want to heal the land ... and I want you.

77.   EXT. BATTLEMENTS. PENDRAGON CASTLE. DAY.

MERLIN and NIMUE walk, hand in hand, on the battlements, looking ecstatically happy. TWO bored GUARDS stand some distance away. MERLIN breathes in deeply.

They look out over the battlements and she points to the distant hills.

> NIMUE:
> Way over there, beyond those hills is an island called Avalon. Joseph of Aramithea came there, from Jerusalem, with the Holy Grail, the cup our Lord Jesus Christ used at the Holy Supper. It has the power to feed the hungry and heal the sick ... But the Holy Grail was lost to us. Many men have searched for it but no-one has seen it since. But one day a man with a pure heart will find it and peace and happiness will return ...

> MERLIN:
> It's a lovely story, and so are you ...

They kiss.

> OLD MERLIN'S VOICE:
> Oh, they hurt ... memories ... memories of love ... they hurt ...

MERLIN and NIMUE walk happily along the battlements while down below, VORTIGERN'S ARMY prepares for war.

> OLD MERLIN'S VOICE:
> Those were truly the happiest days of my life. Our world was tearing itself to pieces ... hell gaped ... and I didn't care ...

78.   EXT. RIVER BANK. GROUNDS. PENDRAGON CASTLE. DAY.

NIMUE and MERLIN sit picnicking on the bank. The TWO guards doze some distance away as NIMUE charmingly feeds MERLIN strawberries.

OLD MERLIN'S VOICE:
I was happy … that's all that mattered … I should've known it wouldn't last … nothing is forever …

MAB rides by behind them and they ALL instantly fall asleep.

79.   INT. COURTYARD. PENDRAGON CASTLE. DAY.

The great castle gates swing open and MAB enters on horseback. She has on a glittering black dress. She is followed by a TROOP of black-hooded PRIESTESSES, riding WHITE HORSES.

VORTIGERN and his KNIGHTS stand on the top of a flight of steps and watch. MAB dismounts and comes up to greet him.

MAB:
Hail, Vortigern, King of Britain. I am Mab, Queen of the Old Ways …

VORTIGERN:
Why've you come?

MAB:
To show you how to defeat Uther.

80.   <u>INT. THRONE ROOM. PENDRAGON CASTLE. DAY.</u>

MAB and VORTIGERN are in conference.

                    VORTIGERN:
What will this alliance cost me? There's a price for everything.

                    MAB:
The wizard, Merlin, I want him.

                    VORTIGERN:
Merlin is too valuable to me, he has visions.

                    MAB:
Anyone can have visions. Don't you have visions? Don't you
see yourself winning?

                    VORTIGERN:
Always … but this time is different. Why do you want to help
me?

                    MAB:
I'd rather have you on the throne than Uther.

                    VORTIGERN:
Why? I don't believe in your Old Ways.

                    MAB:
You don't believe in anything.

                    VORTIGERN:
I believe in me!

                    MAB:
It's not enough.

                    VORTIGERN:
                (smiling)
I understand. Uther will bring Christianity to the people and
that'll be the end of you … right, you can have your wizard. But
how do I defeat Uther?

                    MAB:
Sacrifice Nimue to the Great Dragon.

> VORTIGERN:
>
> That's not so easy.

> MAB:
>
> Ethics?

> VORTIGERN:
>
> Politics ... I'm holding Nimue hostage so her father won't join
> Uther ...

MAB nods.

81.   <u>INT. CORRIDOR. PENDRAGON CASTLE. DAY.</u>

FRIK stands alone in a corridor. He suddenly changes into the twitching SIR
EGBERT. He runs up and down on the spot for a moment to work up a sweat,
then rushes off.

82.   <u>INT. THRONE ROOM. PENDRAGON CASTLE. DAY.</u>

VORTIGERN paces up and down in front of MAB.

> VORTIGERN:
>
> At the moment, it's impossible ... I can't risk it ...

There is a knock on the door and FRIK disguised as SIR EGBERT is ushered
in, panting.

> FRIK/SIR EGBERT:
>
> Urgent news, sire ... Lord Ardent has defected ... he's joined
> Prince Uther.

> VORTIGERN:
>
> The devil take him! ... It comes convenient, Madam.

> MAB:
>
> For both of us.

> VORTIGERN:
>
> The girl dies.

> MAB:
>
> Let Merlin watch.

VORTIGERN:
I can see you might make a bad enemy … But how do I take him, he's a wizard? Last time I had the advantage of surprise. He won't let that happen again.

MAB:
I've already put him to sleep … Make sure you tie his hands before he wakes …

83.   SCENE OMITTED.

84.   EXT. DRAGON'S LAIR. DAY.

CLOSE SHOT: MERLIN. He opens his eyes and stares around him in horror.

CAMERA BACK to show the scorched landscape around the dragon's cave in a cliff-face. There are the remains of previous sacrifices scattered about - burnt stakes and bones.

MERLIN is tied to a tree. Some yards in front of him, nearer to the cave, NIMUE is chained to a stake.

MERLIN:
Nimue!

Even as he shouts, there is a ROAR from inside the cave and a FIREBALL shoots out of it. Its FLAMES are reflected in NIMUE's face as she screams.

MERLIN frantically tries to free his hands. There is a SLITHERING SOUND and the DRAGON comes out of the cave. The cave's entrance is low and deceptive. The devilish CREATURE seems lifesize at first, but once it is clear of the cave, it EXPANDS to its full MONSTROUS size.
As MERLIN struggles, NIMUE screams again.

CLOSE SHOT: DRAGON. The CREATURE shakes himself, flaps his wings a few times and roars. But as he starts to lumber forward, he is hit solidly in the stomach.

CAMERA BACK. MERLIN is still tied to the tree which he has uprooted and is using as a battering ram. The DRAGON staggers back under the blow, more in surprise than pain.

NIMUE:
Merlin! Watch out!

The DRAGON breathes FIRE. MERLIN jumps aside but the tree he is tied to is set alight.

He runs desperately away with a FLAMING TREE on his back. Seeing a small stream, he plunges into it. He douses the FLAMES but not before they have burnt through his ropes and freed his hands.

He looks up to see the DRAGON has fully recovered and is slowly slithering towards a petrified NIMUE.

MERLIN has an idea. He gestures at the STREAM which is immediately diverted and spreads. It quickly becomes a torrent and washes over the DRAGON's feet.
As the earth turns to thick MUD, the DRAGON looks down. It can hardly raise its feet out of the sticky mud which is acting like quicksand.

As MERLIN moves purposely forward, he gestures again. VINES spring up out of the earth, encircling the DRAGON's feet and legs. Other VINES shoot down from the cliff-face and wrap themselves round the DRAGON's neck and body. The more it struggles, the more it becomes entangled until finally it crashes over.

As MERLIN reaches NIMUE, he gestures a third time and ROCKS fall from the cliff, crashing into the DRAGON as it lies roaring on the ground.

As MERLIN gestures and makes NIMUE's CHAINS fall off, the DRAGON breathes a great FIREBALL towards NIMUE and MERLIN.

As MERLIN dives in front of NIMUE to protect her, she screams. But too late. She is scorched by the FIREBALL. MERLIN catches her as she falls.

The DRAGON is totally encased in THICK VINES. One, round its neck, is strangling the CREATURE. It gasps but the vines tighten remorselessly.

MERLIN has laid the badly burnt NIMUE on the ground. Horrified, he bends down beside her.

He gestures and sure enough RUPERT appears on the crest of the hill and gallops down towards them.

CLOSE SHOT: DRAGON. The DRAGON now incapacitated, watches them leave. He looks sad and almost heroic before he dies.

CLOSE SHOT: MAB. She appears and watches MERLIN leave with NIMUE.

MAB:
(to herself)
Very good, Merlin ... very good ...

OLD MERLIN'S VOICE:
Frik was right, Mab had made me use my powers in the end ...

85.   <u>EXT. THE HILLS NEAR AVALON. PRE-DAWN.</u>

Under a storm-filled sky RUPERT gallops across the dark hills with MERLIN clasping the stricken NIMUE in his arms.

<u>ACT FOUR BREAK</u>

86.   <u>EXT. AVALON. MORNING.</u>

The HORSE with MERLIN still holding NIMUE, crests a hill and there in the distance is the Isle of Avalon, shrouded in morning mist. RUPERT gallops towards it.

87.   <u>EXT. ABBEY. AVALON. MORNING.</u>

RUPERT comes to a halt outside the Abbey. The FATHER ABBOT and OTHERS come out and help MERLIN with NIMUE who is gently carried inside.

88.   <u>EXT. CLOISTERS. AVALON. DAY.</u>

The FATHER ABBOT joins MERLIN who is pacing in the shadows of the cloisters.

> FATHER ABBOT:
> She's very badly wounded. The Sisters are doing all they can ... You must pray with us

> MERLIN:
> Why should I pray to your God if he's going to take her from me?

> FATHER ABBOT:
> This isn't God's work.

> MERLIN:
> No you're right, it isn't.

> FATHER ABBOT:
> Do you know who did it?

> MERLIN:
> (quietly)
> Oh yes, I know ...

89.   SCENE OMITTED.

90.   SCENE OMITTED.

91.   EXT. ESTUARY. AVALON. DAWN.

MERLIN walks across the sand flats . . . he is furious!

                    MERLIN:
        Mab - do you hear me?

Mab takes on the appearance of the incoming tide. The water moves in a strange time-lapse dance.

                    MAB:
        Yes, Merlin.

                    MERLIN:
        You destroyed everyone I love … my mother … Ambrosia … and now Nimue.

                    MAB:
        The end justifies the means … I did it for you … I want you to use the power in you … rise up, dear, dear, Merlin and be great!

MERLIN:
I'll destroy you for what you've done to me!

MAB:
(sadly)
You can't, Merlin … I'll always be too strong.

MERLIN strides across the sand near the rocks of AVALON Island. The sand appears to shift in time-lapse.

MERLIN:
I'll find a way.

MAB:
Never … not ever …

The time-lapse tide washes in around MERLIN's feet. MERLIN stares out to sea.

92.   <u>INT. CORRIDOR. NUN'S CELL. AVALON. DAY.</u>

FATHER ABBOT takes MERLIN along the corridor to NIMUE's room.

FATHER ABBOT:
She's resting now, but the worst is over.

MERLIN:
I'm forever in your debt forever, Father Abbot.

FATHER ABBOT stops outside a cell door and peers up at the number.

FATHER ABBOT:
Ah yes, Number 16 … this is the poor girl's cell.

MERLIN:
This is Number 15, Father ... 15!

He moves on to the next cell door.

FATHER ABBOT:
(muttering)
It's an easy mistake to make ... 15 and 16, very similar ... it's got nothing to do with my eyesight!

93.   INT. NIMUE'S CELL. ABBEY. AVALON. DAY.

NIMUE lays on a bed, her face partly bandaged. MERLIN sits beside her and holds her hand. It is difficult but she tries to speak.

MERLIN:
Hush, don't say anything ... save your strength.

NIMUE turns away to hide her wound.

MERLIN:
Don't turn your face to the wall ...

NIMUE speaks in a hoarse, croaking whisper.

NIMUE:
I'll ... be ... scarred ...

MERLIN gently turns her face to him. NIMUE's eyes have filled with tears.

MERLIN:
All that matters is you're alive.

NIMUE forces a brave smile.

MERLIN:
I have to go away for a little while, ... When I come back, it'll be forever... you'll always be beautiful to me.

He bends down and gently kisses her wounded face.

94.   EXT. COUNTRYSIDE. DAY.

MERLIN furiously gallops past on RUPERT, charging through a winter landscape of bare trees and snowdrifts.

95.   EXT. FROZEN LAKE. DAY.

MERLIN rides up to the enchanted lake, its surface covered with ice. Quickly dismounting, MERLIN stands on the shore and looks into the icy lake. Through a patch of clear ice he sees the LADY OF THE LAKE.

> MERLIN:
> Lady it is I, Merlin. You said once you would help me if you could. I need that help now. I need a sword, a great sword.

> LADY OF THE LAKE:
> What for?

> MERLIN:
> To defeat Vortigern. He is Mab's ally, and he has become a tyrant.

> LADY OF THE LAKE:
> The cause is just, I give you Excalibur.

> V.O.:
> It is the sword of the Ancient Kings, it is enchanted, it can only be used for good purpose.

MERLIN walks out across the ice. As he takes the SWORD, the HAND sinks back into the water.

MERLIN weighs the SWORD in his hand and then swings it from side to side. As he does so the SWORD "sings". It is like the plucking of harp strings. We see the figure of MERLIN, on the ice, in the middle of the lake, whirling the flashing SWORD round and round his head to the eerie sound of a harp.

> DISSOLVE TO:

96.   INT. HALL. WINCHESTER CASTLE. DAY.

PRINCE UTHER is a darkly handsome young man with a commanding presence, but also a wild streak which reminds us of his mad father King Constant.

He is in conference with his KNIGHTS and LORDS. Prominent amongst them is the big, blustering SIR BORIS, with his fierce handle-bar moustache and the cool, detached, DUKE OF CORNWALL.

A SERVANT shows MERLIN across the room to UTHER. The SERVANT whispers to UTHER.

UTHER:
You're welcome to Winchester Castle, Merlin.

CORNWALL:
Are you Merlin, the Wizard?

SIR BORIS:
Wizard?! We're all Christians here! We don't believe in your blasphemy, sir!

MERLIN:
That's your choice, sir. But Christian or Pagan, I hope you believe in fresh news.

UTHER:
Is it good or bad?

MERLIN:
It depends how you use it ... Vortigern will attack you within day.

The NOBLES laugh loudly.

CORNWALL:
No-one fights in the winter.

SIR BORIS:
It isn't done, sir! Rules of war. We fight in the summer and rest in the winter. It's tradition!

MERLIN:
Vortigern isn't interested in rules or tradition. He wants to win. If circumstances were different, I'd back him ... His army's already on the march, take it or leave it.

But UTHER is beginning to take MERLIN seriously.

UTHER:
Why're you telling me this?

MERLIN:
Vortigern is the friend of my enemy, Mab, so the enemy of my enemy is my friend ... Besides I've seen the Red Dragon defeat the White and I think you might make a fair to decent king.

UTHER is amused at MERLIN's presumption.

UTHER:
You think so, do you?

MERLIN:
King Constant wasn't, you'll have to do better than your father ... I offer you my services as a wizard.

UTHER:
You take risks, Merlin.

MERLIN:
I'm not here to flatter with a courtier's oily tongue but to serve - not you, but the cause of peace and good government ...

UTHER:
And you sting, Merlin ... but I like the look of you.

SIR BORIS:
But, sire, we're Christians! You can't take a wizard into your service ... it smacks of ... of heresy!

MERLIN:
If my being a wizard offends, take me on as a soldier.

UTHER thinks for a moment, then roars with laughter and grasps MERLIN's hand.

UTHER:
As a soldier!

97.   EXT. FROZEN RIVER. WINCHESTER. DAY.

It is snowing as MERLIN walks out onto the river which is iced over. He tests the thickness of the ice every few yards.

UTHER rides up with SIR BORIS and CORNWALL. MERLIN beckons them out to join him on the ice. UTHER hesitates for a moment, then rides his HORSE across to MERLIN. SIR BORIS and CORNWALL follow.

>UTHER:
>Merlin, I owe you an apology, you were right about Vortigern.

>SIR BORIS:
>What a fool, fighting in winter.

>UTHER:
>Perhaps I was the fool, thinking winter would make me safe … but we'll be ready for him now.

>CORNWALL:
>We must choose our battleground, sire.

>MERLIN:
>Here … we meet him here.

>UTHER:
>You mean by this river?

>MERLIN:
>On it! … he has to come down through the pass and cross here to get to Winchester … Uther, this is where you meet and defeat him!

A cold wind blows, sending scurries of snow swirling round the THREE MEN.

98.   EXT. VORTIGERN'S CAMP. DAY.

MAB rides through the camp to VORTIGERN's tent. SIR GILBERT and SIR EGBERT and his other SOLDIERS turn away in fear as she passes.

99.   INT. VORTIGERN'S TENT. CAMP. DAY.

VORTIGERN puts on his jerkin and pours himself some wine.

MAB:
Uther knows you're going to attack. He's waiting for you.

VORTIGERN:
Who told him I was coming?

MAB:
Merlin.

VORTIGERN:
The Dragon didn't kill him? ... And Nimue?

MAB:
She's alive.

VORTIGERN laughs and drinks.

VORTIGERN:
So much for your magic! ... I never believed in it.

MAB:
That's your only weakness. You don't believe in the Old or the New Ways.

VORTIGERN:
I believe in this!

He raises his fist into her face.

MAB:
It isn't enough.

VORTIGERN:
I've been king for twenty years ... Here's proof ...

He shows her the scars covering his chest.

VORTIGERN:
Every scar a battle fought and won. I've never been beaten and I did it without magic, Pagan or Christian.

MAB:
You're a brave man, Vortigern, but stupid. You must believe in something now!

VORTIGERN:
In you?

MAB:
No - this.

She gives him a small talisman.

VORTIGERN:
This bauble?

MAB:
It'll protect you.

VORTIGERN:
I know the smell of fear. I've been with it all my life. And you're frightened, Madam. The world is passing you by, leaving you and your magic behind ... Old Ways, new Ways, it's all one to me. I've beaten you all and I'll do it again!

He flings the talisman into a brazier. The flames spark and flare and it's gone.

MAB:
Vortigern ... Vortigern ... it's your pride, your damnable pride that condemns you ... I can't save you, but there's one last, precious gift I'll give you free ... I promise you, I won't let you grow old.

100.   EXT. SNOWY FIELD. WINCHESTER. DAY.

CLOSE SHOT: MERLIN. He stands on a rock, head bowed, his hands resting on the handle of the sword EXCALIBUR, upright in front of him. The sound of marching MEN.

CAMERA BACK to show UTHER'S ARMY riding past, led by UTHER. KNIGHTS, ARCHERS, PIKEMEN and MEN-AT-ARMS, turn the snowy field to mud and slush as they trudge on towards the great battle, holding high a forest of Red Dragon banners.

ACT FIVE BREAK

101.   EXT. FROZEN RIVER. WINCHESTER. DAY.

UTHER'S ARMY has taken up positions on a ridge above the frozen river.
Standing alongside UTHER is LORD ARDENT, NIMUE's father, SIR BORIS
and CORNWALL. The FOOT SOLDIERS carry Red Dragon banners.

Suddenly, there appears on a ridge on the other side, a line of White Dragon
banners. Then VORTIGERN'S WHOLE ARMY pours over the ridge with
VORTIGERN, who is mounted, leading them. Flanked by SIR GILBERT and
SIR EGBERT, they take up positions on the river bank.

MERLIN in on a high promontory, looking down at the opposing ARMIES.

VORTIGERN sees LORD ARDENT by UTHER's side.

                    VORTIGERN:
        Ardent! ... The Traitor! He has changed sides!

There is a sudden, tremendous volley of arrows from UTHER's side and
SIR EGBERT gets an arrow in the chest.

                    SIR EGBERT:
        I wish I could.

As he falls dead, UTHER'S and VORTIGERN'S ARMIES charge across the
frozen river at each other. UTHER and VORTIGERN remain on the ridges.

There is a thunderous CRASH as the TWO ARMIES clash head-on in the
middle of the river. The KNIGHTS skid and slide as they hack at each other.
ARCHERS on the periphery of the fighting try to find a firm foothold so they
can unleash their arrows. But mostly it is brutal, hand-to-hand fighting in
appalling conditions.

The SOLDIERS find it more and more difficult to keep their feet on the ice,
which turns treacherously slippery with their blood. The ice and snow quickly
turn red.

UTHER dismounts together with SIR BORIS, CORNWALL and LORD
ARDENT and runs down the slope. As the carnage continues, we see
VORTIGERN still mounted suddenly charge down the slope. UTHER tries to
fight his way to him but there are too many in front of him.

Though SIR GILBERT falls, VORTIGERN's army is winning. There is no
sign of MERLIN as VORTIGERN's army slowly but surely presses UTHER's
men back across the river.

VORTIGERN suddenly spots LORD ARDENT and charges angrily toward him but VORTIGERN's horse slips and he is thrown. He scrambles up and kills LORD ARDENT with one sword blow.

As UTHER is defended by CORNWALL and SIR BORIS, MERLIN enters the battle.

He walks straight across the ice towards VORTIGERN, ignoring the fighting going on on either side of him. When VORTIGERN'S MEN try to attack him, MERLIN doesn't lose his stride. EXCALIBUR flashes in the winter sun and the ATTACKERS are struck down where they stand.

MERLIN reaches VORTIGERN, who turns and sees him.

VORTIGERN:
Are you going to use magic against me, Merlin?

MERLIN:
Yes, I'll kill you any way I can, Vortigern ... but I will kill you.

VORTIGERN laughs and charges at Merlin. As his sword lashes down, Merlin parries it and Vortigern's sword breaks the moment it touches, EXCALIBUR.

VORTIGERN looks on in astonishment. MERLIN raises EXCALIBUR and brings it down hard. But he misses VORTIGERN. As the tip of the sword hits the ice there is a piercing noise like a GUN SHOT. A CRACK snakes its way out from under VORTIGERN's feet across the ice.

The CRACK quickly widens into a fissure. VORTIGERN gives a cry of rage but can't stop himself falling into it. His hands try to grasp the ice but it's too late, he falls into the dark.

The FISSURE immediately closes over him and we see VORTIGERN floating, DEAD, face up, under the ice.

As VORTIGERN'S TROOPS quickly surrender, a great cheer goes up.
UTHER comes over to MERLIN.

> UTHER:
> That's a mighty sword.

> MERLIN:
> It's Excalibur …

He offers the sword to UTHER who takes it reverentially.

> MERLIN:
> It can only be used by a good man in a good cause.

> UTHER:
> I understand …

As UTHER'S MEN crowd round to congratulate him on his victory, MERLIN
slips away.

MERLIN walks away across the icy battlefield, past DEAD and DYING MEN.
There is blood everywhere.

> OLD MERLIN'S VOICE:
> I thought I could now spend time with Nimue … I thought Uther
> would be a good king and so help defeat Mab … but I was never
> a good judge of men … I always expected too much from
> them …

102.   INT. THRONE ROOM. PENDRAGON CASTLE. DAY.

Solemn organ music as the assembled COURT watch UTHER being installed
as king.

A BISHOP reverentially places the crown on his head.

> COURTIERS:
> Long live the king … long live King Uther!

A CHOIR sings joyfully as LORDS and LADIES are presented to the new
KING.

> OLD MERLIN'S VOICE:
> I didn't have to wait long to find out just how wrong I was …

The DUKE OF CORNWALL comes forward to present his beautiful wife, IGRAINE and his small daughter MORGAN LE FEY, who has a cast in one eye, to UTHER.

> CORNWALL:
> Your Majesty, may I present my wife, the Lady Igraine and my daughter …

IGRAINE and MORGAN LE FEY make deep curtsies.

Then everything goes into SLOW MOTION for a moment.

CLOSE SHOT: UTHER. He stares overwhelmed by her beauty.
CLOSE SHOT: IGRAINE. As she stands there we see the figure of MAB, standing provocatively behind her. Nobody else in the room sees MAB, not even MERLIN.

CAMERA BACK and we return to NORMAL SPEED as MAB vanishes.

UTHER licks his lips as he devours IGRAINE with his eyes. Embarrassed, she looks away.

> UTHER:
> You are welcome to Winchester, my lady and you, Miss …

MORGAN LE FEY, a silent, serious child, curtsies again.

> MORGAN LE FEY:
> Morgan le Fey, Your Majesty.

> UTHER:
> Cornwall, will you permit me to dance with your lady after the feast?

CORNWALL has seen UTHER's look and is none too pleased at the request, but he cannot refuse.

> CORNWALL:
> If Your Majesty pleases.

> UTHER:
> Oh yes, it'll please Your Majesty very much.

As CORNWALL escorts his FAMILY away, UTHER can't keep his eyes off IGRAINE and beckons to MERLIN.

> UTHER:
> Igraine … she's beautiful isn't she?

> MERLIN:
> Beautiful and somebody else's wife.

> UTHER:
> But still beautiful ... what does the rest matter?

As UTHER turns to greet OTHERS, MERLIN moves over to MORGAN LE FEY.

> MORGAN LE FEY:
> Are you really a wizard?

> MERLIN:
> So they say.

> MORGAN LE FEY:
> Do some magic for me.

MERLIN smiles, bends down and takes a GOLD COIN out of MORGAN LE FEY's ear. But she doesn't laugh.

> MORGAN LE FEY:
> That's not true magic. It's a trick … anyone can do it.

> MERLIN:
> Anyone? You do it then.

He bends down to make it easier for her. MORGAN LE FEY doesn't notice MERLIN make a tiny gesture with his hand as the LITTLE GIRL reaches up and takes FOUR GOLD COINS out of his ear. She laughs in delight.

> MORGAN LE FEY:
> There you see … I did it!

> MERLIN:
> (smiling)
> You're right, anyone can do it.

He looks up to see UTHER still staring across at IGRAINE. CORNWALL is getting more and more angry.

OLD MERLIN'S VOICE:
He hardly had the crown on his head before it began all over
again ... I decided to leave and let them stew in their own juices

103.   EXT. COURTYARD. PENDRAGON CASTLE. DAY.

As the castle gates open and MERLIN mounts his horse, RUPERT, to leave,
UTHER rides up.
UTHER:
May I ride with you?

MERLIN looks puzzled, but nods.

104.   EXT. ROCKY HILLSIDE. DAY.

MERLIN and UTHER ride along a path beside a rocky hillside.

UTHER:
I believe in you, Merlin.

MERLIN:
And I in you, Uther.

UTHER:
How great is your power? Can you make a woman love me?

MERLIN:
No ... Magic can't create love.

UTHER leans towards him.

UTHER:
Could you kill her husband?...

MERLIN understands what he is talking about.

UTHER:
Igraine ... I want her, Merlin. More than I've ever wanted
anything in the world.

MERLIN:
You can't have her.

UTHER:
Do you know what love is, Merlin?

MERLIN:
Yes, Uther, sad to say I know what love is …

UTHER:
Give me Igraine.

MERLIN:
She's not mine to give.

UTHER:
Then I'll take her, even if it means war.

MERLIN:
It will.

UTHER:
So be it! … I have Excalibur.

MERLIN doesn't reply, then pulls up his HORSE and dismounts.

MERLIN:
Very well, give me the sword … I'll make a spell.

UTHER dismounts and gives him EXCALIBUR. MERLIN holds the sword above his head, then in one swift movement, drives it into a rock. SPARKS fly and the sword shimmers as MERLIN drives it home.

The ROCK moves as the force of the sword wakes the MOUNTAIN KING.

The face of the MOUNTAIN KING appears in the ROCK.

MOUNTAIN KING:
Who dares wake me?

MERLIN:
I am Merlin …

CLOSE SHOT: MOUNTAIN KING

MERLIN'S VOICE:
I've come to ask you for something.

CLOSE SHOT: MOUNTAIN KING

MOUNTAIN KING
Never ask me for anything, I might give you what you deserve.

CAMERA BACK TO INCLUDE MERLIN

MERLIN:
This is Excalibur.

MOUNTAIN KING:
How did you get it?

MERLIN:
A gift from the Lady of the Lake.

MOUNTAIN KING:
She's been a friend since ... since before the dawn of time ... before the dawn of time ... if I can remember that, it means I'm getting old.

The MOUNTAIN KING laughs and the rock rumbles.

MERLIN:
I ask you to hold Excalibur for me, till a good man takes it from you.

The MOUNTAIN KING laughs again and the rock rumbles and pieces fall off.

MOUNTAIN KING:
A good man ... then I will be holding it forever... or even longer.

He stretches out his ROCKY FIST, encasing EXCALIBUR in stone.

UTHER:
You tricked me, Merlin!

MERLIN:
Come, come, Uther, I'm a wizard, that's my business ... the sword is yours if you can take it.

UTHER runs to EXCALIBUR and tries to pull it from the ROCK. It won't budge. UTHER tries again. The sword doesn't move.

UTHER:
Merlin! Where are you, Merlin?!

But MERLIN has already gone, as UTHER tries again and again to pull the sword from the stone.

105.   EXT. HILLS. NEAR AVALON. SUNRISE.

MERLIN rides RUPERT to the crest of hill as the sun rises behind him.

> MERLIN:
> Journey's end, Sir Rupert.
> RUPERT:
> I hope so ...

They ride down towards the Isle of Avalon.

106.   INT. CLOISTERS. ABBEY. AVALON. DAY.

MERLIN and NIMUE walk along the shadowy abbey cloisters. Even though NIMUE' face is heavily veiled, she still keeps to the shadows.

> MERLIN:
> I saw your father die bravely.

> NIMUE:
> It doesn't matter to me how he died. I only know I weep for him.

> MERLIN:
> I killed Vortigern.

> NIMUE:
> You say that almost sadly, Merlin.

> MERLIN:
> No, not after what he did to you ... but when a brave man dies - even one like Vortigern - it leaves a gap.

> NIMUE:
> And Queen Mab?

> MERLIN:
> That will take longer, but I'll do it in the end, I swear.

NIMUE puts her scarred hand on MERLIN's arm.

> NIMUE:
> Don't do it for my sake, Merlin ... to spend your life on revenge is a waste ...

107.   INT. NIMUE'S CELL. ABBEY. AVALON. DAY.

NIMUE sits opposite MERLIN. She pulls her chair a little to one side so she is deeper in shadow.

> NIMUE:
> I'm not ready for you to see me.

> MERLIN:
> Let me be the judge of that.

He deliberately pulls off her veil to reveal her terrible scars.

NIMUE:
I'm a monster.

MERLIN:
No, you're my Nimue.

MERLIN hasn't reacted in any way to the sight of her scarred face. He is too busy concentrating.

Keeping his eyes focused on her face, he makes a distinctive gesture with his right hand.

Nothing happens. Her face remains scarred. MERLIN becomes more and more desperate as he tries again and then again. Still nothing happens. NIMUE quietly feels her face. She knows the scars remain.

MERLIN:
(distressed)
I can't do it... Mab is too strong.

NIMUE puts the veil back on.

OLD MERLIN:
I wanted it so much ... it was the most terrible moment of my life ...

MERLIN:
Leave this place and come with me.

NIMUE:
I'm not ready to face the world.

MERLIN:
When will you be ready?

NIMUE:
I don't know...

MERLIN:
First Ambrosia ... then you ... now Uther ... I've lost you all ... I am in hell! ... What do I do? ... Help me, Nimue!

NIMUE and MERLIN embrace.

NIMUE:
Look into your heart, my dearest. You'll find a way.

ACT SIX BREAK

108.   EXT. UTHER'S CAMP. TINTAGEL CASTLE. DAY.

Tintagel Castle sits on a rocky promontory connected to the mainland by a narrow causeway. A small detachment of SOLDIERS can easily defend it.

UTHER'S ARMY is camped on a cliff on the other side of the causeway. UTHER is outside his tent, staring angrily at the castle. He turns to SIR BORIS.

> UTHER:
> Three months siege, and we still haven't taken it!

> SIR BORIS:
> There's no way across the causeway, sire … My advice is to give it up, it's madness.

> UTHER:
> I must have Igraine.

> SIR BORIS:
> As one who's been to Colchester and know a few things, I have to tell you sire, the kingdom is falling apart while we tear ourselves to pieces. If you were fighting for more land, more money, more power, I could understand it … but all this for a woman?! …

> UTHER:
> You were born old, Boris. You've never known what it is to lust after a woman. I've spent all my life fighting … bloody days and cold nights with a naked sword as a bedfellow - now I want something warmer.

> SIR BORIS:
> You'll never take Tintagel.

UTHER reacts as he sees MERLIN riding into camp.

109.   INT. UTHER'S TENT. DAY.

MERLIN confronts UTHER.

MERLIN:
Hundreds're dead because you have an itch.

UTHER:
Will you help cure me of that itch?

MERLIN:
You're reputation's gone, Uther and reputation, like glass, once its cracked, can't be repaired.

UTHER:
Will you help me?

MERLIN:
I don't know you anymore. You've become an Uraboros - a serpent whose eyes're the colour of blood, whose teeth're cut like saws, whose tail shoots poisoned darts ... you'll devour the world in your lust!!

UTHER:
(relentlessly)
Will you help me?!

MERLIN:
Yes ...I have to be made to stop this madness.

UTHER:
What will it cost me?

MERLIN:
You will have Igraine, but there'll be a child ... a boy ... I've seen him. Uther, he's mine!

UTHER:
What'll you do with him?

MERLIN:
Teach him honour and goodness.

UTHER:
I can do that.

MERLIN:
"Honour" ... "Goodness" ... the words stick in your throat Uther ... you choke on them, just as you'll choke on your own vomit in the end.

UTHER bites his lip in rage, but he needs MERLIN.

UTHER:
Very well, I agree.

MERLIN:
Once more ... Cornwall will not be harmed!

UTHER:

Not by me.

MERLIN gestures and a CRYSTAL ORNAMENT appears on the table. It spins slowly, catching the light.

MERLIN:

That's there to remind you … Now, break camp … withdraw your army. Do it now, in daylight, so Cornwall can see.

110.   EXT. UTHER'S CAMP. TINTAGEL CASTLE. SUNSET.

UTHER has broken camp and is riding away at the head of his ARMY.

111.   EXT. BATTLEMENTS. TINTAGEL CASTLE. SUNSET.

CORNWALL and some of his MEN watch UTHER'S ARMY ride away.

CORNWALL:

Saddle my horse. We'll follow him.

IGRAINE and MORGAN LE FEY join him.

IGRAINE:

Don't leave, my lord.

CORNWALL:

Why not?

IGRAINE:

I have a feeling.

CORNWALL:

The castle's well guarded … you'll be safe, my love … Look after your mother, Morgan.

MORGAN LE FEY:
(seriously)

I will, Father.

112.   EXT. TINTAGEL CASTLE. SUNSET.

CORNWALL leads some of his MEN out of the castle and across the causeway, following UTHER. GUARDS immediately lower the portcullis behind them.

113.   EXT. HILL OVERLOOKING TINTAGEL CASTLE. SUNSET.

CLOSE SHOT: MERLIN and UTHER. The TWO on horseback, watch CORNWALL leave, from the distant hilltop.

> MERLIN:
> Night is your friend ... use it.

He gestures and UTHER turns into CORNWALL. Realising what has happened, UTHER laughs loudly.

CAMERA BACK as he gallops away down the hill towards the castle and across the causeway.

The horse, RUPERT, neighs.

> MERLIN:
> You don't approve?

> RUPERT:
> Of course I don't approve.

> MERLIN:
> The ends justify the means.

> RUPERT:
> Where have I heard that before?

CLOSE SHOT: MERLIN. He realises the truth of RUPERT's comment.

114.   EXT. TINTAGEL CASTLE. SUNSET.

UTHER as CORNWALL rides up to the gates. The GUARDS look surprised at "CORNWALL"'s quick return.

> UTHER/CORNWALL:
> Open the gates!

The GUARDS raise the portcullis and UTHER/CORNWALL rides in.

115.   INT. IGRAINE'S BEDCHAMBER. TINTAGEL CASTLE. DUSK.

IGRAINE, in a nightgown, is at her mirror, brushing her golden blonde hair, whilst MORGAN LE FEY plays with her dolls.

UTHER/CORNWALL come in.

> IGRAINE:
> Back so soon, my lord?

> UTHER/CORNWALL:
> Yes, yes, Uther's really gone … My place is here with you.

CLOSE SHOT: MORGAN LE FEY. She stares fixedly at UTHER/ CORNWALL.
CLOSE SHOT: UTHER. MORGAN LE FEY sees UTHER not CORNWALL.

CLOSE SHOT: MORGAN LE FEY. She isn't fooled.

> MORGAN LE FEY:
> Mother …

CAMERA BACK to show UTHER/CORNWALL sweating. He senses MORGAN LE FEY knows who he really is so he sweeps her up into his arms.

> UTHER/CORNWALL:
> Time for you to go to bed, little lady … not another word …

He deposits her outside and locks the door.

> IGRAINE:
> Oh, I didn't say "goodnight" …

UTHER/CORNWALL kisses her passionately.

> UTHER/CORNWALL:
> (huskily)
> Goodnight … goodnight and then goodnight …

He kisses her again.

116.   EXT. GORGE. ROCKY LANDSCAPE. DUSK.

CORNWALL, pierced by dozens and dozens of arrows like a grotesque pin-
cushion, lied dead amid his slaughtered ARMY. He is in the middle of a sea of
DEAD BODIES.

117.   INT. UTHER'S TENT.DUSK.

CLOSE SHOT: SPINNING CRYSTAL. The CRYSTAL given by MERLIN to
UTHER, left in the deserted tent, slowly stops spinning NOQ CORNWALL is
dead. It then slowly falls apart.

                    OLD MERLIN'S VOICE:
        Things fall apart they say ... I knew what Uther had done, but I
        made myself believe good could come of it in the end. And a
        child would be born ...

118.   INT. IGRAINE'S BEDCHAMBER. DAY.

IGRAINE is in labour, attended by her WOMEN.

119.   INT. MAB'S SANCTUM. DAY.

MAB sits brooding on her throne, whilst FRIK, looking like an ancient scholar,
writes in a large book.

                    MAB:
        What're you doing?

                    FRIK:
        Writing fairy stories ... so you'll be remembered.

                    MAB:
        I don't need to be remembered, Frik, I won't be forgotten.

                    FRIK:
                    (doubtfully)
        Hhmm ...

                    MAB:
        Things're going well for us?

FRIK:
They certainly seem to be.

MAB:
I'm going to make sure.

120.   INT. HALL. TINTAGEL CASTLE. DAY.

MORGAN LE FEY is playing with her dolls. There is a gentle knocking on the door. It opens and FRIK peers in.

FRIK:
Hello, Morgan.

FRIK slips in and closes the door behind him.

MORGAN LE FEY:
(startled)
Who're you?

FRIK:
I'm a gnome.

MORGAN LE FEY:
You're tall for a gnome aren't you?

FRIK:
Gnomes come in all shapes and sizes. I'm the tall kind.

MORGAN LE FEY:
Can you do magic?

FRIK:
Of course … watch.

He transforms himself into a handsome, swashbuckling Errol-Flynn-like CHARACTER.

He bows gallantly to a delighted MORGAN LE FEY.

FRIK:
Ah, beautiful lady, I am at your service, your wish is my command!

He jumps up onto the table and flourishes his sword.

FRIK:
Watch me swash a buckle!

MORGAN LE FEY laughs happily as FRIK jumps down and transforms himself back into his original BUTLER.

MORGAN LE FEY:
That's real magic, not tricks. Will you teach me how to do that?

FRIK:
Certainly, if you do something for me. Your new baby brother will be born soon.

MORGAN LE FEY:
He's not my real brother. The man who made him wasn't my real father.

FRIK:
That's very clever, Morgan. You'll make a very good pupil for all the wonderful things I can teach you ...

MORGAN LE FEY:
What do you want me to do?

FRIK takes a rune stone out of his pocket.

FRIK:
Just put this stone in the baby's crib.

MORGAN LE FEY nods and takes the stone.

121.   EXT. CLIFF-TOP. SEA SHORE. TINTAGEL.DAY.

MERLIN stands on a cliff-top. There is a massive cliff-tower, which has split off from the shore, rising out of the sea.

OLD MERLIN'S VOICE:
I thought it was going to be a new beginning ...

122.   INT. IGRAINE'S BEDCHAMBER.DAY.

IGRAINE writhes in the bed, still in labour.

123.   EXT. CLIFF-TOP. SEA SHORE. TINTAGEL.DAY.

MERLIN still stands on the cliff-top.

                    OLD MERLIN'S VOICE:
          I could only see Igraine in labour. I was blind to everything
          else …

124.   INT. MORGAN LE FEY'S ROOM. TINTAGEL.DAY.

MORGAN LE FEY sneaks into the nursery and hides the rune stone in the
BABY's crib.

125.   INT. IGRAINE'S BEDCHAMBER.DAY.

IGRAINE gasps and the CHILD is born. It is slapped. It cries out lustily as a
NURSE holds him up.

126.   EXT. CLIFF-TOP. SEA SHORE. TINTAGEL.DAY.

MERLIN looks out at the ocean.

                    OLD MERLIN'S VOICE:
          And so Arthur was born …

                    MERLIN:
          At last … a good man, a good king!

The terrifying figure of MAB takes shape on the cliff-tower opposite. She
shouts across at MERLIN. The clouds above them move at incredible speed.

                    MAB:
          You're easily fooled, Merlin! Uther did it when he killed
          Cornwall. His child is damned.

                    MERLIN:
          The boy's mine!

The SEA below, between the two rocks, boils and rages.

                    MAB:
          He'll be his father's son! Because of him, the chaos of blood
          will go on and on and out of it the people will come back to me!

MERLIN hurls the words across the raging chasm.

MERLIN:
I'll see you fade into nothing!

MAB:
Poor Merlin wrong again ... I'M WINNING!

As the waves below crash and thunder, she disappears. The moment she does, the SEA grows CALM. The sky plunges into NIGHT.

A beautiful moon comes out from a cloud behind MERLIN

MERLIN:
You see Mab! ... The future is <u>bright</u>! ...

FADE OUT.

<u>END OF PART ONE</u>

PART II

INSERT

200. <u>CLOSE SHOT: OLD MERLIN.</u> This is the traditional OLD MERLIN of the opening scene of Part One, with a white beard.

> OLD MERLIN:
> Where was I? … Oh yes, oh yes … Arthur had just been born … I fostered him with Sir Hector and his own son, Kay.

201. <u>SCENE OMITTED.</u>

202. <u>INT. ROOM. SIR HECTOR'S CASTLE. DAY.</u>

The boy, ARTHUR sits at a desk, being lectured by MERLIN and watched by SIR HECTOR.

> OLD MERLIN'S VOICE:
> I was his Tutor … I didn't teach him magic, I taught him ethics, morals … which is much more difficult, believe me …

BOY ARTHUR suppresses a yawn.

203. <u>INT. THRONE ROOM. PENDRAGON CASTLE. NIGHT.</u>

A prematurely OLD UTHER sits on the throne in the dark, deserted throne room, trembling.

> OLD MERLIN'S VOICE:
> Uther went mad, like his father and killed himself …

204. <u>INT. CHURCH. PENDRAGON CASTLE. NIGHT.</u>

OLD UTHER plunges a dagger into his chest and falls across a candle-lit altar.

OLD MERLIN'S VOICE:
That bring us up-to-date, I think ...

205.   EXT. COUNTRYSIDE. DAY.

MERLIN and ARTHUR, now the young man we had seen earlier, are riding together through rocky hillsides.

OLD MERLIN'S VOICE:
I'd told Arthur the true history of his birth and we were riding to claim his birthright ...

206.   EXT. EXCALIBUR VILLAGE. DAY.

CLOSE SHOT: EXCALIBUR. It is still stuck deep into the rock. BEEFY HANDS grab it and pull. It doesn't budge.

CAMERA BACK to show a KNIGHT tugging furiously at the sword. Other KNIGHTS and LORDS surround him, jeering and waiting their turn to try.

A whole village has spring up round the sword in the rock. Now it is crowded with CONTENDERS for the sword and the vacant throne.

The VILLAGERS are cashing in on the event. Giant pies, cooked meats and barrels of ale are being sold from trestle tables, whilst PEDDLERS cry their wares, selling religious knick-knacks; Christian and Pagan.

Amongst the LORDS, milling about the rock are the aristocratic SIR HECTOR, his grown-up son, KAY and SIR BORIS, older but still blustering.

SIR BORIS:
Stand back! This is a job for a man!

He downs a tankard of ale, burps loudly and spits on his hands. Grabbing the sword handle, he pulls with all his strength. His face turns red, his neck muscles bulge but the sword doesn't move.

VILLAGE CHIEF:
Is that wind bag back again?

VILLAGE WOMAN:
If he isn't careful he'll do himself an injury!

They all jeer as SIR BORIS finally gasps and collapses with the effort.

207.   EXT. HILLSIDE PATH. DAY.

MERLIN and ARTHUR continue to ride.

                    ARTHUR:
          If I'm Uther's only son, I want what is mine. I want to
          be king.

                    MERLIN:
          And if you are king, what then?

Before ARTHUR can answer, MERLIN's horse, RUPERT, suddenly
stops. MERLIN stops ARTHUR's HORSE.

                    ARTHUR:
          What is it?

He half-draws his sword, expecting a trap but MERLIN points to a
SNAIL crossing the path in front of them.

                    MERLIN:
          He has the right of way.

ARTHUR looks bewildered but waits with MERLIN.

                    MERLIN:
          You were saying ... if you were king ...

                    ARTHUR:
          I'd do the things you taught me ... Build a golden city
          called Camelot, devoted to peace and charity.

He looks down into the exquisite valley. A lake glistens far below.

                    MERLIN: *
          The world needs justice and compassion more than
          charity ... But Camelot sounds like a dream worthy of a
          king, Arthur.

The SNAIL has crossed out of harms way.

                    ARTHUR:
          Let's hurry.

As he urges his HORSE forward, in his haste he breaks a BRANCH off a overhanging tree.

MERLIN stops under it and pushes it back into place. It miraculously heals itself and MERLIN rides on after the impetuous ARTHUR.

208.   <u>SCENE OMITTED</u>

209.   EXT. EXCALIBUR VILLAGE. NIGHT.

The village is asleep. A few LORDS and KNIGHTS remain but they are drunk or asleep too.

MERLIN and ARTHUR ride in and up to the sword in the rock. They dismount and ARTHUR touches EXCALIBUR.

>   ARTHUR:
>   It's more beautiful than they say.

>   MERLIN:
>   All the knights in Britain have tried to take it … it is the sword of
>   the king … it's yours, Arthur.

As ARTHUR grasps the sword, there is a rumble and the FACE of the MOUNTAIN KING appears in the rock.

>   MOUNTAIN KING:
>   Who is it?... Merlin?... It seems you were only here a moment
>   ago.

>   MERLIN:
>   This man claims Excalibur.

>   MOUNTAIN KING:
>   Another idiot who blows out the light to see how dark it is.

>   ARTHUR:
>   I'm Arthur, the only son of Uther and rightful king of Britain.

At that moment a nearby ROCK splits and MAB appears.

>   MAB:
>   Why give him the sword? He'll betray the people, just as his
>   father did.

ARTHUR:

I don't know what I'll do or what I'll become. I only know what
I _am_!

MOUNTAIN KING:

A good answer.

ARTHUR looks at MERLIN.

ARTHUR:

I had a good teacher.

MAB:

He will try to destroy the Old Ways. You'll be forgotten like the
rest of us. It'll be as if you'd never existed.

MOUNTAIN KING: *

That's your fear not mine, Mab. What transforms and
transcends isn't courage or faith but loss. I can't die. I'm the
rock of ages. It doesn't matter to me if I'm forgotten or not. I'll
live forever, on the edge of dreams...

MERLIN:

Now, Arthur!

ARTHUR hesitates for a moment. MERLIN gives him an encouraging look
and ARTHUR begins to pull the SWORD inches out of the rock.

MOUNTAIN KING:

The sword is yours.

He releases his grip. MAB smiles sardonically and causes the SWORD to glow
red hot. ARTHUR hangs onto it and continues pulling through the pain.

Blood drips from his hands as ARTHUR pulls the SWORD from the stone.

The FACE of the MOUNTAIN KING disappears as an exultant ARTHUR
holds the gleaming EXCALIBUR high, whilst blood from his wound drips
onto his head.

ARTHUR:

Excalibur!

MAB:
(smiling)
Look at him Merlin, his reign begins in blood and will end the
same way.

She vanishes and MERLIN crosses to ARTHUR to embrace him.

VILLAGERS and KNIGHTS have been woken by the noise and start tentatively to gather round ARTHUR and MERLIN.

ARTHUR holds up EXCALIBUR. The OTHERS look on in awe.

> VILLAGE CHIEF:
> He has the sword ... he has Excalibur!

> FIRST VILLAGER:
> He's the king!

As the VILLAGERS drop on one knee to pay homage to ARTHUR, the VILLAGE CHIEF whispers to the FIRST VILLAGER

> VILLAGE CHIEF:
> That's the end of us ... with no sword nobody's got any reason to come here ... this village is dead ...

The other VILLAGERS haven't realised what the loss of EXCALIBUR means and shout:

> VILLAGERS:
> Long live the King! Long live the King!

ARTHUR laughs in triumph.

209A   SCENE OMITTED

210.   INT. CHAPEL. WINCHESTER. DAY.

UTHER'S CORPSE is laying in state in the chapel, surrounded by candles. LORDS and KNIGHTS are supposedly paying their last respects but instead are quarreling bitterly over who should now become king.

LORD LOT, a stern inflexible noble and his son, GAWAIN, are shouting at SIR BORIS, SIR HECTOR, and his son, KAY, and the small fiery LORD LEO.

> LORD LOT:
> Uther was my cousin! ... I claim the throne by right.

LORD LEO:

You didn't pull Excalibur from the rock!

LORD LOT:

Nobody did!

GAWAIN:

If someone had, I'd follow him even against my father. But you all failed. My father is king by right of blood!

LORD LEO:

I am nearer to Uther than you.

SIR HECTOR:

His sister was Uther's niece ... I pledge my army to Lord Leo!

LORD LEO:

Listen to Sir Hector.

SIR BORIS:

I have a claim too!

GAWAIN:

Nobody's going to follow a bearded blow-hard!

SIR BORIS gives a roar of anger and the NOBLES are at each other's throats. The fighting is so fierce they don't notice they accidentally knock UTHER'S CORPSE off its slab.

At the height of the shouting and fighting, MERLIN and ARTHUR come in. MERLIN gestures and all the NOBLES lose their voices. They keep shouting but make no sound. Immediately they stop fighting.

Having got their attention, MERLIN stands in the middle of the chapel with ARTHUR.

MERLIN:

That's better isn't it, my lords? Now you can listen instead of fighting which should be a novel experience for most of you... Uther had a son ... I give you, Arthur, the true king of Britain.

MERLIN gestures as ARTHUR steps forward and the NOBLES recover their voices.

LORD LOT:

Uther had no son.

LORD LEO:
Everyone knows that!

SIR BORIS:
He did have a son.

Whilst the OTHERS look surprised, ARTHUR quickly picks up UTHER's body and puts it back on the slab.

SIR BORIS:
When Uther conquered Tintagel and took Lady Igraine, a son was born. It's true - I was there.

SIR HECTOR:
Merlin brought the boy to me to raise … He's Uther's son.

GAWAIN:
If he is, let him draw Excalibur from the stone.

ARTHUR:
I already have!

He unsheathes EXCALIBUR and holds it high.

GAWAIN:
Prove it! Prove that it is Excalibur.

ARTHUR swings the sword round which snuffs out ALL the CANDLES.

SIR BORIS finally moves forward and kneels on one knee in front of ARTHUR.

SIR BORIS:
You have Excalibur and you're Uther's son … I acknowledge you as my liege lord and king.

SIR HECTOR:
So do I.

LORD LEO also kneels.

LORD LEO:
He has the sword. Accept him, Lot ... Arthur is king.

LORD LOT:
No ... never ... I'll not bend my knee to a boy. Nor will my son.

GAWAIN:
I can speak for myself, father ... He has Excalibur. He is the king.

LORD LOT:
Gawain! You'd go against your own father?!

GAWAIN:
If the cause is just.

LORD LOT:
And if it's not, and you're wrong?

GAWAIN:
Then you'll have to kill me in battle ... I'm the king's man, father.

LORD LOT:
(coldly)
So be it!

MERLIN:
Please, my Lords, hard as it may be for you, think a moment ... we've seen too many wars.

LORD LOT:
My mind's made up!

He storms out with OTHER NOBLES.

ARTHUR takes MERLIN aside.

ARTHUR:
(whispering)
Speak to them.

MERLIN:
(whispering)
That's your job now ... you are the king.

ARTHUR turns to THOSE who are left.

> ARTHUR:
> My lords, I accept your allegiance with gratitude ... I hope, that Lord Lot will not make war against us. I want to bind up this nation's wounds. But if he does, we'll be ready. Our cause is just, our arm strong and we will win.

The chapel resounds with the cheers of the NOBLES. Only MERLIN looks grim, he knows what is in store.

211.   INT. MAB'S SANCTUM. DAY.

MAB is looking into a CRYSTAL. It drains of colour and she throws it on a pile of colourless discarded crystals in one corner.

> MAB:
> Don't you ever tidy up, Frik?

FRIK, in his butler mode, appears from behind a GIANT CRYSTAL.

> FRIK:
> I try, Your Majesty, but I'm overworked and I can't use imps, gnomes or fairies, they're useless when it comes to anything practical. I've so much to do ...

> MAB:
> And you'll have more ... I've given up on Merlin ... I thought perhaps, despite everything, he would come round in the end...

> FRIK:
> He's a very stubborn creature.

> MAB:
> I wanted him to, so I fooled myself.

> FRIK:
> I've never known you to do that before over anyone.

> MAB:
> Enough of this! ... Arthur's cursed ... I want to make sure everyone knows in time... that's going to be your job, Frik.

212.   <u>EXT. BATTLEMENTS. TINTAGEL CASTLE. DAY.</u>

MORGAN LE FEY, now a young woman, is on the battlements. She still has a cast in one eye and is still playing with toys of a kind - she is flying a black kite which swoops and soars high above her. She is so busy watching it, she doesn't notice FRIK appear behind her.

                    FRIK:
        Hello, Morgan ... My, you've grown.

MORGAN LE FEY turns.

                    MORGAN LE FEY:
        Who're you?

                    FRIK:
        Don't you remember me? I used to visit you when you were
        very young ...

FRIK changes himself into the handsome swashbuckling ERROL FLYNN FIGURE, jumps up on the narrow wall of the battlements and "tightropes" his way along them.

MORGAN LE FEY smiles.

                    MORGAN LE FEY:
        I remember you ... I thought you were a dream.

                    FRIK:
        I'm real ...

                    MORGAN LE FEY:
        You lied to me. You told me you'd make me beautiful and you
        never did.

FRIK jumps off the battlements in front of her.

                    FRIK:
        Did I? Then I will ... but first you must put away childish
        things.

He produces a pair of shears and cuts the kite string of MORGAN LE FEY's kite. The kite is swept up and away into the blue. MORGAN LE FEY looks up at it sadly.

FRIK:
Why so sad? It's only a toy.

She smiles and turns back to him to see he is holding up a hand mirror.

FRIK:
Look at yourself …

CLOSE SHOT: HAND MIRROR. MORGAN LE FEY sees her reflection in the
mirror. She is still plain.

But subtly her IMAGE begins to CHANGE and she becomes very beautiful.
She has no cast in her eye. It is the same young woman, only very lovely.
She is thrilled at the transformation.

MORGAN LE FEY:
I'm beautiful!

FRIK:
Very, very beautiful... I think clothes, cut in the Roman style are
the only gowns for a lady of fashion.

MORGAN LE FEY:
It's wonderful… Now get me the throne!

FRIK:
That's beyond my powers …

As they walk back along the battlements, the black kite, already a tiny dot in the
sky, is finally lost from sight.

213.   INT. GREAT HALL. TINTAGEL CASTLE. DAY.

MORGAN LE FEY and FRIK are seated, drinking wine from goblets and
laughing.
FRIK:
I can tell you from personal experience, elves're so short, when
it rains they're the last to know…

The shape of the drinking goblet he is holding changes into MAB'S face.

MAB:
(hissing)
Stop enjoying yourself and get on with it!

The face vanishes. FRIK becomes serious.

> FRIK:
> I've been thinking, my lady, there might be a way of giving you what you want … Your <u>son</u> could be king.

> MORGAN LE FEY:
> How? If Arthur defeats Lord Lot, he'll be king and I can't marry him.

FRIK sits beside her and whispers seductively.

> FRIK:
> You don't have to marry him to have his son.

> MORGAN LE FEY:
> We have the same mother.

> FRIK:
> And underneath this charming, devastatingly handsome exterior I'm a crabby old gnome …

He kisses her passionately on the mouth.

> FRIK:
> Does it matter?

> MORGAN LE FEY:
> Not a bit … you don't have to seduce me to win me over … like everybody else I want the crown!

> FRIK:
> I like you, Morgan le Fey - you're an honest young woman.

> MORGAN LE FEY:
> And I like you, whoever you are.

They kiss passionately.

214.   <u>SCENE OMITTED.</u>

215.   <u>EXT. ARTHUR'S CAMP. OVERLOOKING BATTLEFIELD. DAY.</u>

ARTHUR'S ARMY is now camped and resting on a hill overlooking the battlefield.

SIR BORIS joins ARTHUR, MERLIN and GAWAIN.

SIR BORIS:
The army's almost ready, sire. It's going to be a bonny fight!

He is obviously looking forward to it. The OTHERS are not. SIR BORIS leaves them.

MERLIN:
You know why yours father's fighting us, Gawain, don't you?

GAWAIN:
Yes, he's doing it for me... If he wins, he'll be king. And then the crown would pass to me … that's what he really wants …

ARTHUR:
Ah...

GAWAIN:
But I don't want it!

SIR BORIS rejoins them.

SIR BORIS:
We're ready, sire. Will you give the order?!

ARTHUR looks across at MERLIN, who seems to know what he is thinking. MERLIN nods.

Without giving the order, ARTHUR mounts his HORSE.

ARTHUR:
Wait for my signal.

He rides out alone towards the battlefield.

LORD LEO:
What the devil's he doing?!

SIR HECTOR:
He'll be killed … Merlin!

But MERLIN remains silent.

216.   <u>EXT. GREEN BATTLEFIELD. DAY.</u>

ARTHUR rides slowly across the battlefield.

217.   <u>EXT. LORD LOT'S CAMP.</u>

LORD LOT and the other LORDS and their KNIGHTS wait in astonishment as ARTHUR slowly rides up.

The KNIGHTS lower their lances and the ARCHERS their bows.

ARTHUR stops in front of LORD LOT and dismounts.

> ARTHUR:
> There's no reason why men should die today, my Lord. The quarrel is between us.

> LORD LOT:
> It is.

ARTHUR unsheathes EXCALIBUR.

> ARTHUR:
> This is Excalibur, the sword of the true king. If you believe you have a right to it … take it …

He hands EXCALIBUR to LORD LOT.

ARTHUR:
And kill me.

He drops on one knee in front of LORD LOT.

LORD LOT swings the sword in his hand for a moment, and raises it high as if to bring it down in ARTHUR.

He suddenly stops as he feels the swords magic.

LORD LOT:
Forgive me, Arthur … I can feel it ... the sword is yours …

He raises ARTHUR up.

LORD LOT:
You are the true king … The war is over!

His MEN cheer and lay down their banners and their arms. Their cheers are taken up by ARTHUR'S ARMY on the other side of the battlefield as they realise what has happened.

SIR BORIS, SIR HECTOR and MERLIN gallop across to join them. LORD LOT gives EXCALIBUR back to ARTHUR.

LORD LOT:
Arthur is our true king by blood and right!

GAWAIN rides up, jumps off his HORSE and embraces his FATHER.

Other KNIGHTS ride up and surround ARTHUR in a circle.

ARTHUR:
Here in this circle, let us give thanks to the Saviour for this deliverance. And let this circle be a symbol of our purpose. Each man in it is equal to the other, each has a voice, each will strive to fight for truth and honour … Let us pray.

ALL kneel as ARTHUR holds up EXCALIBUR.

CLOSE SHOT: MERLIN. He doesn't pray. He has no part in this but he approves of what ARTHUR has done.

218.   EXT. ARTHUR'S CAMP. EVENING.

SOLDIERS are resting on the ground after the battle. OTHERS are drinking and eating as MERLIN saddles his horse, RUPERT.

ARTHUR comes out of his tent.

                    ARTHUR:
              You're leaving us, Merlin?

                    MERLIN:
              I'm going to see Nimue.

                    ARTHUR:
              How can you bear it? To love her so much and not be with
              her?...I'd never be content with that.

MERLIN smiles sadly.

                    MERLIN:
              You're still young ... You'll learn ...

He mounts his HORSE.

                    ARTHUR:
              God be with you, Merlin.

                    MERLIN:
              Hhmm, yes, of course ... but it's more important He
              be with you, Arthur.

He rides away.

219.   EXT. COUNTRYSIDE. NEAR ARTHUR'S CAMP. EVENING.

The beautiful, bejewelled MORGAN LE FEY is at the head of a party of her SERVANTS, riding to pay their respects to the new King. FRIK rides beside her, dressed as a rich, handsome NOBLEMAN.

220.   EXT. HILLS OUTSIDE ARTHUR'S CAMP. NIGHT.

MERLIN rides up a hill some miles from ARTHUR's camp. He looks back to see the camp fires burning brightly. From a line of flaming torches he knows VISITORS are entering the camp but he can't see who they are.

> OLD MERLIN'S VOICE:
> I thought I'd finally achieved one of my dreams … at last there was a good king on the throne …

He rides on.

221.   EXT. ARTHUR'S CAMP. NIGHT.

It is FRIK and MORGAN LE FEY who are the Visitors to ARTHUR's camp. Lit by torches, the procession makes its way through the camp. MEN and WOMEN on all sides watch them as they pass and finally stop in front of ARTHUR's tent.

As MORGAN LE FEY is helped down from her horse by FRIK, ARTHUR comes out of his tent with SIR BORIS, LORD LOT and GAWAIN.

FRIK sweeps off his hat and bows low.

> FRIK:
> Your Majesty, I present my Lady Marie, Queen of the Border Celts, who comes to pay you homage.

MORGAN LE FEY curtsies and ARTHUR extends his hand.

> ARTHUR:
> You are most welcome, my lady.

222.   INT. ARTHUR'S TENT. CAMP. NIGHT.

FRIK and MORGAN LE FEY have just come in with the   OTHERS. As MORGAN LE FEY stands in the soft lamplight, ARTHUR sees for the first time how beautiful she is. He is stunned.

Only FRIK sees MAB standing behind MORGAN LE FEY for a brief moment, smiling at ARTHUR's reaction. She quickly vanishes.

SIR BORIS and the other NOBLES in the tent are more interested in the rich gifts MORGAN LE FEY'S SERVANTS bring in for the new king than in ARTHUR's reaction.

MORGAN LE FEY smiles at him but says nothing. Embarrassed, ARTHUR clears his throat.

> ARTHUR:
> Lady, we are overwhelmed by your gifts … We'd like to entertain you but we're moving back to Pendragon in the morning.

> MORGAN LE FEY:
> (softly)
> Perhaps I and my servants can join you for the night… We've had a long, tiring journey and would like to rest before we return home.

> ARTHUR:
> (eagerly)
> Of course! … We can spend time together … you can tell me about your people! …

CLOSE SHOT: MORGAN LE FEY. She smiles warmly.

> MORGAN LE FEY:
> It will be my pleasure, Your Majesty.

223.   INT. ARTHUR'S TENT. CAMP. NIGHT.

ARTHUR and MORGAN LE FEY laugh and whisper intimately together.

223A.   EXT. ARTHUR'S TENT. CAMP. NIGHT.

The camp echos with a WOMAN'S soft, mocking laughter.

> OLD MERLIN'S VOICE:
> They didn't hear Mab's laughter … she wasn't laughing at them … she was laughing at me …

224.   <u>INT. COURTYARD/GARDEN. ABBEY. AVALON. DAY.</u>

MERLIN has managed to persuade the still veiled NIMUE to come out in the
sunlight, into the neglected, overgrown patio of an inner courtyard to find the
FATHER ABBOT asleep on a grassy bank. A CAT stretches out in the warm
sun nearby.

MERLIN and NIMUE sit on a grass verge. MERLIN picks a tall dandelion
puff-ball and gently blows on it. The SEEDS disperse in the air and float away.

We follow ONE SINGLE airblown SEED as it floats round the patio on the
gentle currents of air.

>   NIMUE:
> I can't stand the thought of other people ... peering ...
> whispering ... pointing at me.

>   MERLIN:
> We can live in the forest ... animals don't whisper or point.

>   NIMUE:
> It's a dream, Merlin.

>   MERLIN:
> I want to make it real.

The CAT stretches out a lazy paw to catch the SEED but it floats past till it
hovers over the sleeping FATHER ABBOT. As he breathes out, he sends the
SEED spinning away and then breathes in, pulling the seed towards him till it
ends on the tip of his nose.

>   NIMUE:
> I found a peace here Merlin, in prayer and meditation ... it's a
> peace I've never known before ... it passeth all understanding.

>   MERLIN:
> It passeth my understanding Nimue ... Why are you shutting
> yourself away?

>   NIMUE:
> So I can be nearer to my God.

>   MERLIN
> The nearer you are to Him the further you are from me. Will
> you take off the veil?

NIMUE:

No.

MERLIN:

Good, then I can ...

MERLIN stretches out to remove the veil. She tries to stop him by pushing his hand away but he is determined. She turns her face away but he gently forces it back.

He bends down and gently kisses her. She turns away again.

225.   INT. ARTHUR'S TENT. CAMP. NIGHT.

ARTHUR is making love to MORGAN LE FEY on the bed. He bends over and kisses her passionately.

226.   INT . NIMUE'S ROOM. AVALON. NIGHT.

MERLIN sleeps in a chair whilst NIMUE is still asleep on the bed. MERLIN wakes with a start and sees the hot wax from the burning candle bubbles then change into the melting miniature shapes of ARTHUR and MORGAN LE FEY. The tiny figures melt, writhe and flow into each other.

MERLIN:

What're you showing me Mab… What've you done?

MAB'S laughter grows until it fills the room.

ACT ONE BREAK

227.   SCENE OMITTED.

228.   EXT. ESTUARY. AVALON. MORNING.

MERLIN rides furiously away from the Abbey, across the causeway, through the morning mist.

OLD MERLIN'S VOICE:

I rode fast that day… but I knew I was already too late to stop an act that could destroy us all.

229.   EXT. FORECOURT. PENDRAGON. CASTLE. DAY.

MERLIN gallops into the forecourt of Pendragon Castle.

230.   INT. THRONE ROOM. PENDRAGON CASTLE. DAY.

ARTHUR is in conference with some NOBLES, including SIR BORIS and SIR HECTOR.

MERLIN bursts in.

MERLIN:
Out, my lords!

The NOBLES look resentful but ARTHUR signals for them to leave. As they exit, MERLIN shouts at SIR BORIS.

MERLIN:
And close the door behind you!

ARTHUR:
What's the matter, Merlin?

MERLIN:
Tell me the truth, Arthur ... two nights ago you slept with a woman.

ARTHUR:
Yes, if you must know, I did. Though I don't see why I should have to tell you.

MERLIN:
Who was she?

ARTHUR:
I don't like the question, Merlin.

MERLIN:
Who was she?!

ARTHUR:
Marie, Queen of the Border Celts.

MERLIN:
No, that was Morgan Le Fey.

ARTHUR:
Uh?

MERLIN:
Her mother was the Lady Igraine - your mother.

ARTHUR slumps onto the throne, stunned.

ARTHUR:
But I didn't know, I swear I didn't know ...

MERLIN:
There'll be a child, Mab will see to that ... He'll be the future and he'll destroy us!

231.   INT. MAIN HALL. PENDRAGON CASTLE. NIGHT.

MAB dances in triumph to unheard music in the moonlit room. FRIK is seated on the dais next to the throne and smiles only when MAB looks in his direction, otherwise he is miserable.

232.   EXT. BATTLEMENTS. PENDRAGON CASTLE. NIGHT.

MERLIN climbs up onto the battlements and looks up at the night sky in rage and despair.

Thunderclouds gather and he finds himself creating a TERRIBLE STORM.

There are suddenly claps of thunder and fork lightning splits the sky. The expression on MERLIN's face tells us these are the emotions he is experiencing as all his hopes seem to have been destroyed.

It pours with RAIN but MERLIN doesn't notice as he stands, an isolated figure on the battlements in the middle of a MIGHTY STORM.

233.   INT. AVALON ABBEY. COURTYARD/GARDEN. NIGHT.

MAB appears in the deserted patio and leaves a small broken mirror on the grass before vanishing as NIMUE enters.

NIMUE sits on the ground and immediately sees the mirror glinting in the grass. She picks it up.

CLOSE SHOT: NIMUE. She looks at herself in the broken mirror. Her face in the mirror is still terribly scarred. But the face subtlety changes. The scars disappear and she becomes the beautiful woman she was, again.

CAMERA BACK to show MAB standing beside her.

                    NIMUE:
          I wondered where this came from.
          There are no mirrors in Avalon

                    MAB:
          You see how I can change you?

                    NIMUE:
          You already have, you scarred my face.

                    MAB:
          I'm sorry, it was unfair.

NIMUE:

It was evil.

MAB:

With evil all around me, there's nothing I can do that isn't evil, to survive.

NIMUE:

No, that's too easy, you have to fight it, like Merlin.

MAB:

It's because of Merlin all this happened.

NIMUE:

That's not true ... why're you here, Mab?

MAB:

To make you an offer. I'll restore your beauty if you'll take Merlin away to a place I've created for you. You can live with him there till the end of your days ...

NIMUE:

And be happy?

MAB:

And be happy.

NIMUE:

He has a destiny, Mab. It would keep him from his purpose.

MAB:

It would keep him from wasting his life.

NIMUE:

He believes fighting for what is right isn't a waste, ... I wouldn't do that to him ... I love him.

MAB:

I love him.

NIMUE:

You hate him.

MAB:

I hate him, too ... What's your answer?

                              NIMUE:
     No.

                              MAB:
     I'm sorry if you change your mind just speak my name aloud.

     She vanishes. NIMUE picks up the broken mirror and looks at herself again.
     She has changed back, the terrible scars have returned. She breaks down and
     cries.

                         OLD MERLIN'S VOICE:
     But the darkest hour, they say, is before dawn...

234.   EXT. CAMELOT. DAY.

     The city of Camelot is being built, on a beautiful site, of rolling hills and
     glorious countryside.

     There are tents and marquees and building equipment everywhere.

234A.   EXT. COURTYARD. CAMELOT. DAY.

     A surprised MERLIN rides through the CROWDS of WORKERS as ARTHUR
     comes out of a golden pavilion.

                              ARTHUR:
     Merlin! …

     He jumps down from the pavilion and runs over to MERLIN as he dismounts.

                              ARTHUR:
     It's good to see you, old friend. I wasn't sure you'd come
     after that terrible night at Pendragon …

                              MERLIN:
     What's all this, Arthur?

                              ARTHUR:
     A promise made flesh. I'm building the city of Camelot.

     They walk towards the pavilion.

                              ARTHUR:
     It's a new beginning … I made a mistake that night with Morgan
     but I don't believe I'm condemned for all eternity for one
     mistake.

MERLIN:
Not by me, Arthur ... I'll never condemn you.

There is an awkward pause as they re-establish their friendship.

ARTHUR:
I hope to marry Lord Leo's daughter.

MERLIN:
Ah ... do you love her?

ARTHUR:
She'll be a splendid Queen and a good wife.

MERLIN:
(quizically)
The question is, Arthur, will you be a good husband?

ARTHUR:
I'll try ... yes.

MERLIN embraces him warmly.

ARTHUR:
We'll be married here at Camelot. I don't care it's not
finished ... will you be there with me?

MERLIN:
I'd be honoured. What's your bride's name?

ARTHUR
Guinevere.

235.   INT. CAMELOT. GREAT HALL DAY.

Organ music booms out. The hall is crowded for the wedding. A vivid colourful
scene with LORDS and LADIES in their glittering robes. But the hall is still
under construction. There is no glass in the windows and the roof is open to the
skies.

MERLIN and GAWAIN stand beside ARTHUR at the altar in
front of the presiding ARCHBISHOP.

The organ music suddenly stops and the doors burst open to reveal the stunningly lovely figure of GUINEVERE, dressed in white, standing in bright sunlight.

The organ music starts up again as she walks down the aisle, followed by her father, LORD LEO and SIR BORIS.
The CONGREGATION gasps at her beauty as she walks slowly to the altar, where she slips her arm through ARTHUR's. He is a little stiff and awkward but EVERYONE is enchanted by her except MERLIN, who is distinctly uneasy. He senses something is wrong but he doesn't know what.

As the BRIDE and GROOM kneel in front of the ARCHBISHOP, the sun passes behind a cloud and there is a sudden summer shower. NO-ONE takes any notice and the ceremony continues.

236.   INT. GREAT HALL. CAMELOT. NIGHT.

MERLIN meets ARTHUR in the deserted throne room.

                    ARTHUR:
        What is it, Merlin?

                    MERLIN:
        I've a gift for you, Arthur ... You remember after you defeated
        Lord Lot, all the Knights stood in a circle and you talked of
        equality and justice?

                    ARTHUR:
        I remember.

MERLIN takes something out of his pocket. It is a tiny wooden TABLE with roots like a tree.

                    MERLIN:
        You see, it's a perfect circle ... if you plant it in Camelot it will
        grow ... it will come to symbolise everything we stand for ...

ARTHUR is enchanted with the tiny TABLE.

                    ARTHUR:
        Thank you, Merlin ... I'll try not to disappoint you again.

                    MERLIN:
        We all make mistakes, even wizards. Perhaps wizards most of
        all.

ARTHUR:
I will atone for my sin with Morgan... One day I'll find the Holy Grail, I swear.

237.   <u>SCENE OMITTED.</u>

237A.   <u>EXT. CAMELOT. DAY.</u>

                             OLD MERLIN'S VOICE:
               And so the year past and it seemed that Guinevere had brought
               the priceless gift of happiness to Camelot ...

238.   <u>INT. CAMELOT. GREAT HALL. DAY.</u>

GUINEVERE joins MERLIN in the Great Hall.

GUINEVERE:
I hear you're leaving us, Merlin?

MERLIN:
I have things to do for Arthur ...

They walk toward the door.

MERLIN:
I'd like to ask you a question before I go.

GUINEVERE:
Anything ... you're my friend as well as Arthur's.

MERLIN:
Do you love him Guinevere?

GUINEVERE:
Yes, I do.

MERLIN:
Ambrosia used to say "Love - that's the most important thing".
And she was right ... she was always right.

GUINEVERE:
Arthur keeps talking about going on a quest for the
Holy Grail.

Merlin nods.

MERLIN:
But not just yet ... not until I find a man to take his place while
he's away.

GUINEVERE:
Don't search too hard, I don't want to lose him.

MERLIN:
Oh, he'll be back.

GUINEVERE:
I don't want to spend my life waiting.

MERLIN thinks of NIMUE.

MERLIN:
Yes ... yes .... I can understand that.

GUINEVERE:
You asked me if I loved him ... does he love me?

MERLIN:
Good heavens, woman, don't you know?

GUINEVERE:
I'm not sure ... You're a wizard, Merlin, look into Arthur's heart and tell me if he loves me.

MERLIN:
The heart is the one place that's hidden from me, Guinevere.

239.   EXT. HILLSIDE ABOVE CAMELOT. DAY.

MERLIN and RUPERT, crest the hill above Camelot. The horse, sighs.

RUPERT:
Another long journey, Merlin?

MERLIN:
Yes, I'm sorry, Sir Rupert ...

240.   EXT. TINTAGEL CASTLE. DAY.

The castle stands on a rocky windswept cliff.

OLD MERLIN'S VOICE:
I was going to see Morgan le Fey ... But honestly I didn't know what I expected to achieve ...

241.   INT. HALL. TINTAGEL CASTLE. DAY.

MORGAN LE FEY is happily playing with her sweet-looking two-year-old son, MORDRED when a MAID comes in.

MAID:
Merlin is here to see you, my lady.

MORGAN LE FEY:

Send him in.

The MAID leaves and MORGAN LE FEY picks up MORDRED.

MORGAN LE FEY:

You hear that, Mordred, there's a wizard come to see us. Won't this be fun?

MORDRED gurgles happily and MERLIN comes in.

MERLIN:

Lady Morgan ... you know why I'm here?

MORGAN LE FEY:

Say hello to my son, Mordred.

MERLIN:

Master Mordred.

MORDRED makes a rude noise with his mouth. MORGAN LE FEY frowns.

MORGAN LE FEY:

That was rude, Mordred. You can do anything you like, but you must never be rude ... "rude" is being weak.... You were saying, Merlin?

She puts MORDRED down.

MERLIN:

You know why I'm here?

MORGAN LE FEY:

It's to do with my son ... Hasn't he grown?

MERLIN:

Yes, more than is natural.

MORGAN LE FEY:

Of course, it's magic.

MERLIN:

Oh ... I beg you, for the country's sake, don't teach him the Old Ways.

MORGAN LE FEY:
This country means nothing to me. A bastard sits on the throne.
A bastard begot in blood when his father, Uther, seduced my
mother and killed my father.

MERLIN:
It's the future I'm thinking of ...

MORGAN LE FEY:
You would think of the future, Merlin, because the past is too
painful ... It was you! You chose Uther to be king, you helped
him seduce my mother and destroy me. In the end you begot
Mordred just as surely as Queen Mab and Arthur!

MERLIN:
I know, but I can live with it.

MORGAN LE FEY:
Just as you'll have to live with the fact Mordred will be king.

MERLIN:
No, that can't be ...

The little MORDRED, who has been playing, suddenly flings a knife at
MERLIN, who catches it just before it hits him in the heart.

MORGAN LE FEY:
(indulgently)
Mordred ... Mordred ... Merlin is a guest ... don't be naughty
... He just wants attention ... you'll get all the attention you want
when you're king, dear ...

MERLIN:
What about the Old Ways?

MORGAN LE FEY:
You're in no position to lecture me on what I can do or can't do
... The Old Ways've been good to me ... they've given me a son
and made me beautiful.

MERLIN:
It's only an illusion.

MORGAN:
Beauty is always only an illusion, Merlin, didn't you know?

MAB and a handsome FRIK come in straight through the door.

MAB:
We thought we'd come in the traditional way, by the door.

MERLIN:

You're supposed to open it first.

MORGAN LE FEY:
Mordred, here's your Auntie Mab and your Uncle Frik.

MORDRED rushes over to MAB and jumps into her arms. She whirls him round.

MAB:
Sweetie ... sweetie ... I've got lovely toys for you ...

MERLIN:

Mab ...

MAB:
It's good to see you, Merlin.

FRIK:
It's been ages, Merlin. Do you ever think of your old school where I tried to teach you the fundamentals of magic? He could've been my star pupil, Morgan but he proved ...

MAB:
Disappointing ... but you won't will you Mordred?

Frik goes over to MORGAN LE FEY and kisses her gallantly.

MORGAN LE FEY:

Isn't he handsome?

FRIK:
Handsome is as handsome does ... what does that mean? I've never really understood the phrase.

MAB:
Toys, Mordred ... Auntie always brings you toys ...

She stares and a SMALL CROWN appears on MORDRED's head, then A SMALL PONY appears. MORDRED shrieks with delight as MAB puts him on it and leads him round and round the hall. She is obviously besotted with the little BOY.

                    MORGAN LE FEY:
          You see, Merlin, you took my family away from me ... now I
          have a new one.

She kisses FRIK, who responds.

                    MERLIN:
          It won't last, Morgan.

                    MORGAN LE FEY:
          Nothing does.

                    MAB:
          Don't you feel it, see it, Merlin? I'm winning ... I have the
          precious gift of patience ... It'll be years before dear Mordred
          can claim the throne but I can wait ... time means nothing to
          me ...

She picks MORDRED up off the PONY and whirls him round.

                    MAB:
          You'll be the death of Arthur and the end of all of poor Merlin's
          dreams ... won't you, my sweetest?

MORGAN LE FEY and FRIK laugh as MORDRED gurgles agreement. There is nothing MERLIN can do. He turns and walks out of the room.

                    MAB:
          Look, angel, there's nothing the big bad wizard can do. See him
          run ... run wizard, run, run, run ...

MERLIN slams the door behind him, cutting off their mocking laughter.

242.   EXT. LAKE. DAY.

It is Autumn, the leaves on the trees have turned golden as MERLIN comes down to the water's edge and gestures at the DUCKS on the lake.

They start diving under the water, first ONE, then ANOTHER, then ANOTHER. The LADY OF THE LAKE appears out of the depths.

LADY OF THE LAKE:
Merlin? You're troubled again?

MERLIN:
It's still the same cry for help, Lady ... Your sister, Mab, grows more powerful.

LADY OF THE LAKE:
And I grow weaker.

MERLIN:
What can I do? I have to find a man to guard the throne when Arthur goes questing for the Holy Grail. The temptation will be to seize the crown when he's gone.

LADY OF THE LAKE:
You need a man pure in heart.

MERLIN:
I've tried to find him before, but he doesn't exist.

LADY OF THE LAKE:
The answer is at Joyous Gard ... My ship will take you.

She vanishes. In her place, MERLIN sees a ghostly three-masted sailing SHIP, gliding towards him.

243.   EXT. DECK. SAILING SHIP. LAKE. DAY.

MERLIN lies down on the deck asleep as the mysterious SHIP sails on.

OLD MERLIN'S VOICE:
The deserted ship sailed across the enchanted lake to Joyous Gard ... a land of dreams ... but it was a real place with real people ...it was also the future...

ACT TWO BREAK

244.   EXT. DECK. SAILING SHIP. JOYOUS GARD. DAY.

MERLIN is still asleep on the deck. A SHADOW passes over his face. He opens his eyes and looks up to see a golden boy, YOUNG GALAHAD, standing over him. The sun is directly behind him, so he seems to glow.

                    YOUNG GALAHAD:
     Who're you?

                    MERLIN:
     I'm the wizard, Merlin.

                    YOUNG GALAHAD:
     There aren't any wizards left.

                    MERLIN:
     I'm the last of them …

He gets up.

                    MERLIN:
     And who're you?

                    YOUNG GALAHAD:
     Galahad … my mother is the Lady Elaine and my father is Sir Lancelot.

                    MERLIN:
     And this place is?

                    YOUNG GALAHAD:
     Joyous Gard.

MERLIN goes to the side of the ship and looks out to see the castle of Joyous Gard built on the side of the sea.

245.   EXT. COURTYARD. JOYOUS GARD. DAY.

YOUNG GALAHAD leads MERLIN into the courtyard. Everything is different. It seems a place set in the 13th Century with knights in shining armour and ladies in silk robes and long conical hats.

246.   INT. SMITHY. CASTLE. JOYOUS GARD. DAY.

Amid the smoke and flames of a blacksmith's fire are the BLACKSMITH and
LANCELOT, a charismatic figure, perhaps a little too handsome and certainly a
little too complacent. They are honing a gleaming sword. LANCELOT carefully
holds the edge of the sword to a grindstone which the BLACKSMITH slowly
turns.

Satisfied, LANCELOT nods and the BLACKSMITH stops turning the
grindstone.

YOUNG GALAHAD and MERLIN watch LANCELOT test the blade by hitting
it against an anvil and pulling it up to his ear and listening to the reverberations.

                    MERLIN:
            What does it say?

                    LANCELOT:
            It says "I will prove strong and true in battle" ... and to be wary
            of strangers ... Well done Master Blacksmith.

                    YOUNG GALAHAD:
            Father, this is Merlin.

                    LANCELOT:
            Merlin? .. Ah, then you're no stranger, I've heard of you, Sir.
            You're welcome.

As they come out of the smithy into the courtyard Merlin looks around.

                    MERLIN:
            Tell me, what is Joyous Guard?

                    LANCELOT:
            A place which believes in honour and chilvalry ... where the
            strong defend the weak ... it is a glimpse of the future, Merlin.

247.   EXT. GROUNDS CASTLE. JOYOUS GARD. DAY.

LANCELOT and YOUNG GALAHAD lead MERLIN through a beautiful
garden to a glorious bower.

LADY ELAINE sits gossiping with her MAIDS. She is a beautiful WOMAN,
dressed in white.

LANCELOT:
Merlin, this is my wife, Elaine ...

MERLIN bows formally.

MERLIN:
My lady, a great honour.

The MAIDS leave as ELAINE smiles graciously and gestures for MERLIN to sit opposite her in the bower whilst YOUNG GALAHAD sits beside his MOTHER.

ELAINE:
We've heard of you, even here in Joyous Gard.

MERLIN:
It's a beautiful place.

ELAINE:
As close to heaven as we could find on earth. Though I sometimes think my husband finds it just a little too sedate now there are no more tyrants to overthrow or dragons to slay.

LANCELOT:
I slaughtered the last one five years ago.

ELAINE:
(teasing)
And now there are none left he has to fill his days with hunting and early evenings by the fire.

LANCELOT:
(sighing)
I never thought I'd miss dragons.

ELAINE:
You've had a long journey, Merlin. You must be tired and hungry.

MERLIN:
No, I've too much to do ... I've come here to find a man to defend King Arthur in his kingdom ... but he has to be a good man, pure in heart.

ELAINE looks up proudly at LANCELOT.

ELAINE:
You've found him

OLD MERLIN'S VOICE:
It was all too easy … I should've known …

248.   INT. ELAINE'S BEDROOM. JOYOUS GARD. DAY.

LANCELOT in full armour is saying goodbye to ELAINE and YOUNG
GALAHAD.

LANCELOT:
Are you sure this what you want?

ELAINE:
It's not what I want, it's what <u>you</u> want. I can't hold you back.
It's your chance for one last great adventure…

LANCELOT embraces her and they kiss.

ELAINE:
May God keep you safe.

LANCELOT:
Galahad, protect your mother while I'm away.

YOUNG GALAHAD:
Yes, father.

249.   EXT. SHORE. JOYOUS GARD. DAY.

ELAINE has her arm round YOUNG GALAHAD's shoulders as they watch the
SHIP sail silently away across the sea and into the mists.

250.   EXT. GROUNDS. CAMELOT. DAY.

In the grounds in front of the half-finished castle of Camelot, ARTHUR is
holding a tournament.

KNIGHTS in bright armour and richly appareled HORSES ride past, practising with their lances, piercing various targets in front of a CROWD of SPECTATORS.

ARTHUR takes his place on the pavilion with GUINEVERE and other NOBLES.

A trumpet sounds. ARTHUR steps forward.

> ARTHUR:
> I shall leave soon on a God-Given quest for the Holy Grail. Now I seek a champion to protect the country and the honour of the queen while I'm gone!

The SPECTATORS cheer as GAWAIN rides up in front of the pavilion.

> GAWAIN:
> I claim that honour, sire.

> ARTHUR:
> I hope you don't win, Gawain. I need you with me.

ARTHUR sits next to GUINEVERE. SIR BORIS, LORD LOT and SIR HECTOR are seated with them.

> SIR BORIS:
> You should've let me compete in the tourney, sire!

> ARTHUR:
> You're too old, Sir Boris.

> SIR HECTOR:
> Of course he's too old, but I'm not!

As ARTHUR and GUINEVERE laugh, MERLIN and LANCELOT ride onto the jousting field. LANCELOT is in shining armour and has his visor down so no-one can see his face.

> MERLIN:
> Your Majesty, I wish to vouch for Sir Lancelot of the Lake, who wishes to enter the jousts.

ARTHUR and the NOBLES look surprised.

> ARTHUR:
> So be it, Merlin.

He gives a signal, a trumpet sounds, the tournament pennant is raised and the jousting begins. The tournament is a melee and twenty knights collide in a haphazard fray.

251.   EXT. JOUSTING FIELD. CAMELOT. DAY.

TWO KNIGHTS, lances smash into each other, one lance breaks but the other LIFTS the opposing KNIGHT clean off his HORSE and he lands with an almighty crash amid tremendous cheers.

CLOSE SHOT: ANOTHER KNIGHT. He is hit full in the chest and falls.

CLOSE SHOT: GALLOPING HORSE. Nostrils flared, the HORSE races forward to the sound of cheers and crash of lances against armour.

CLOSE SHOT: KNIGHT. A stricken KNIGHT falls INTO FRAME.

CLOSE SHOT: ARTHUR and GUINEVERE. They cheer.

CLOSE SHOT: KNIGHT. He lays, spreadeagled, on the ground.

CLOSE SHOT: LANCELOT. He raises his lance in triumph.

CLOSE SHOT: KNIGHT. He takes a direct hit as he hurtles OFF his HORSE.

CLOSE SHOT: LANCELOT. He is again triumphant.

CLOSE SHOT: GUINEVERE. She claps and cheers.

CAMERA BACK to show there are only TWO KNIGHTS left on the jousting fields, GAWAIN and LANCELOT.

They turn their HORSES.

They ride towards each other, then increase speed, lowering their lances. They end up galloping furiously at each other.

There is a great cheer as they meet HEAD ON, their lances smashing into their opponent. GAWAIN is knocked OFF his HORSE and crashes to the ground, leaving the tip of his lance embedded in LANCELOT's shoulder.

LANCELOT dismounts. He goes over to the fallen GAWAIN and gallantly helps him to his feet.

Amid resounding applause, the TWO KNIGHTS cross to the pavilion and stand before ARTHUR, GUINEVERE, MERLIN and the NOBLES.

> ARTHUR:
> Magnificently done, noble sir.

LANCELOT lifts his visor and GUINEVERE reacts.

Neither she nor anyone else sees MAB materialise behind her and whisper in her ear.

> MAB:
> He's very handsome, isn't he?

> GUINEVERE:
> Yes …

> ARTHUR:
> What did you say, lady?

> GUINEVERE:
> Nothing …

She looks around puzzled but MAB has already vanished.

> LANCELOT:
> Your Majesty, I offer you my sword and my life.

> ARTHUR:
> It is an honour, brave knight.

GAWAIN turns and shouts to the SPECTATORS.

> GAWAIN:
> Lancelot of the Lake takes the honours … he is the best and noblest of the knights!

The SPECTATORS cheer. MERLIN looks pleased.

> ARTHUR:
> As champion, Lancelot, you will wear the Queen's colours.

LANCELOT dips his lance to GUINEVERE. As she bends down and ties her handkerchief to his lance, she sees the blood pouring down his arm and hand.

> GUINEVERE:
> You're wounded, sir.

> LANCELOT:
> A little, my lady ... but let that be our secret.

But suddenly weak from the wound, he sways and slumps to the ground as GUINEVERE cries out.

252.   INT. TENT. JOUSTING FIELD. CAMELOT. NIGHT.

Stripped to the waist, LANCELOT lies on his bed with the end of GAWAIN's lance still in his shoulder. The three PHYSICIANS make preparations as GAWAIN and GUINEVERE come in.

> GUINEVERE:
> How is he?

> CHIEF PHYSICIAN:
> Fair to middling, considering we haven't taken the lance out yet.

> GAWAIN:
> Why not?

> CHIEF PHYSICIAN:
> There is a dispute - a scholarly dispute - as to whether we should take it out con or contra-wise, which means to the mere layman, turning and pulling it to the left or to the right ...

> FIRST PHYSICIAN:
> Contra ... thus the turning and pulling will be in line with the planetary aspects of Jupiter and Mars.

> SECOND PHYSICIAN:
> No, turn and pull con-wise, as the planets Venus and Uranus will be the dominant influences ...

As they argue, GUINEVERE kneels beside LANCELOT.

> GUINEVERE:
> Is there anything I can do for you, Sir Lancelot?

> LANCELOT:
> Hold my hand, lady.

> GAWAIN:
> You're Physicians - instead of arguing about it, do it.

> FIRST PHYSICIAN:
> Do it?! We must talk about it first.

> SECOND PHYSICIAN:
> Indeed ... these are weighty matters, fit only for experts.

> CHIEF PHYSICIAN:
> Trust us! If we treat a knight for a broken arm, that's what he'll die of!

Exasperated GAWAIN crosses to LANCELOT.

> GAWAIN:
> Are you ready, Sir Knight?

> LANCELOT:
> Do it, Gawain.

LANCELOT squeezes GUINEVERE's hand even tighter as GAWAIN bends to remove the splintered lance.

LANCELOT's and GUINEVERE's eyes lock together. Perhaps it is that moment they fall in love?

Without warning, GAWAIN pulls the splintered lance free. LANCELOT gasps with pain and passes out.

253.   INT. ROYAL BEDCHAMBER. CAMELOT CASTLE. NIGHT.

ARTHUR prepares for bed as GUINEVERE looks out of the window at the starry night.

> ARTHUR:
> How is Lancelot?

> GUINEVERE:
> He's past the worst.

> ARTHUR:
> Good ... that's good.

GUINEVERE turns away from the window.

GUINEVERE:
Must you go on this quest?

ARTHUR:
Yes, I must, but not at once.

GUINEVERE:
And if I beg you not to?

ARTHUR:
What's wrong? What're you afraid of, Guinevere?

GUINEVERE:
Nothing ... I'll miss you so.

ARTHUR:
I'll miss you too, but I've given my word ... to God.

GUINEVERE:
I need you more.

ARTHUR:
You'll have Merlin ... and Lancelot.

GUINEVERE:
(fearful)
I know.

ARTHUR can't understand her fear.

ARTHUR:
You'll be safe with them.

He kisses her and she responds passionately as if trying to obliterate her fears.

253A.   EXT. COURTYARD. CAMELOT CASTLE. DAY.

ARTHUR and LANCELOT are walking through the half-completed grounds of
the castle.

ARTHUR:
You have become a friend, Lancelot, when I go, I want you to
see that Camelot is finished just as I planned.

LANCELOT:
Of course I will, sire ... when will you go?

ARTHUR:
Next Spring.

254.   EXT. COURTYARD. CAMELOT CASTLE. DAY.

It is already Spring but Camelot is still only part built though the scale of it is already apparent. ARTHUR and his KNIGHTS are preparing to leave on his quest for the Holy Grail. GAWAIN is with them.

PRIESTS bless the ARMY, sprinkling holy water over HORSES and MEN.

GUINEVERE, LANCELOT and other NOBLES are assembled to say farewell. MERLIN watches them from the steps as CROWDS can be seen outside the gates, cheering and waving.

ARTHUR:
Sir Lancelot, guard the honour of our sovereign lady, the Queen.

LANCELOT:
I will, sire.

GUINEVERE:
Go in God's good grace, my love ... we pray you come back soon.

ARTHUR bends over in the saddle and with one arm round her, pulls her up to him and kisses her. He deposits her gently back onto the ground.

ARTHUR:
Goodbye, Merlin.

MERLIN:
Goodbye Arthur ... come back to us.

ARTHUR:
I leave the country in your hands.

He gives the signal and ARTHUR and his KNIGHTS ride out of Camelot, banners flying .

255.   EXT. BATTLEMENTS. CAMELOT CASTLE. DAY.

GUINEVERE and LANCELOT are standing with MERLIN and the remaining NOBLES looking out across the countryside at ARTHUR and his KNIGHTS riding away.

256.   EXT. SKY. ABBEY. AVALON. DAY.

A DOVE circles over the Abbey at Avalon, then flies down.

257.   INT. NIMUE'S CELL. ABBEY. AVALON. DAY.

The DOVE lands on the window-ledge of NIMUE's cell where MERLIN and NIMUE are arguing.

                        MERLIN:
        You want to stay here for the rest of your life?!

                        NIMUE:
        Yes!

                        MERLIN:
        Why? ... Why?!

                        NIMUE:
        For the love of God.

He takes her in his arms.

                        NIMUE:
        Please don't do that ... when you touch me my faith trembles.

She gets up and goes to the window.

                        MERLIN:
        What about your faith in our love?

                        NIMUE:
        That never weakens ...

She comes back to him and smiles.

                        NIMUE:
        But touch me one more time ... I think my faith can stand it.

258.   INT. HALL. TINTAGEL CASTLE. DAY.

FIVE uniformed SERVANTS are lined up against a wall, each with a RED
APPLE on his head.

They tremble violently as MORDRED, now fully grown , takes aim with his bow from the other side of the room.

MAB, MORGAN LE FEY and FRIK watch him indulgently from comfortable chairs, whilst the family pet, a HAIRLESS CAT lies on the rug in front of the fire with a GRIFFIN in a dog's collar, who is snoozing contentedly.

MORDRED, an extraordinarily cool and arrogant young man, calls out.

> MORDRED:
> If you five gentlemen don't stop trembling, I might miss and kill you all.

The FIVE SERVANTS try desperately to stop trembling. SOME close their eyes as MORDRED takes aim again.

He fires at incredible speed, slicing each APPLE neatly in two, with an ARROW.

But the last SERVANT balancing the apple on his head is trembling so badly MORDRED misses the target.

> MAB:
> Ah, less than perfect.

A petulant MORDRED fires an ARROW at MAB who catches it in mid-air, then ONE at a slower FRIK, who thankfully catches it just an inch away from his throat. MORDRED is about to fire at MORGAN LE FEY.

> MORGAN LE FEY:
> (sharply)
> That's enough, Mordred.

> MAB:
> You mustn't get carried away, my sweet. It shows a lack of control.

> MORGAN LE FEY:
> And why fire at Auntie Mab and Uncle Frik?

> FRIK:
> I hope the boy was just having fun and it wasn't personal.

MORGAN LE FEY:
Of course it wasn't personal ... he likes you.

She kisses FRIK.

FRIK:
I often wonder what he'd do if he <u>didn't</u> like me?

MORDRED:
Stop fussing, Mother ... Aunti Mab understands don't you,
Auntie Mab?

MAB:
Of course I do, you were testing yourself ... come sit by me.

MORDRED sits himself elegantly on the arm of MAB's chair and puts his arm
round her.

MAB:
You know, you're my favourite, Mordred ... but you must learn
to channel your aggression.

MORDRED:
Against Arthur.

MAB:
Of course, always against Arthur ... and Merlin ... You're
looking pale, Mordred, you're not eating enough.

A BANQUET of FOOD and DRINK appears on the table in front of them.
MORDRED fastidiously picks out a small delicacy.

MORDRED:
I already have the strength of ten men.

MORGAN LE FEY:
Listen to your Aunt ... and please do something about your hair.

MORDRED:
Very well, Mother.

MORGAN LE FEY:
There's a good boy.

MORDRED smiles.

259.   EXT. HILLSIDE ABOVE CAMELOT. DAY.

A MESSENGER gallops over the ridge towards Camelot.

260.   SCENE OMITTED.

261.   INT. ROYAL APARTMENTS. CAMELOT. NIGHT.

A MESSENGER presents letters to Guinevere.

MESSENGER:
My lady… letters from the King!

A fire blazes in the huge fireplace as LANCELOT, GUINEVERE and MERLIN
read the letters ARTHUR has sent to them.

As GUINEVERE reads, she sees ARTHUR'S FACE in the FLAMES of the FIRE.

ARTHUR'S VOICE:
We are no nearer finding the Holy Grail than when we left …
We hear rumour it's housed in the next town … and the next …
and the next … and each town takes us further away from you
and Camelot … I need the Grail and I need you, my love …

GUINEVERE lays the letter to one side.

> LANCELOT:
> Why so sad, my lady?

> GUINEVERE:
> Because it's winter … because Camelot is cold and empty
> without him.
> LANCELOT:
> Let me build up the fire.

He puts a log on the fire.

> MERLIN:
> He'll be back.

> GUINEVERE:
> Does he say when?

> MERLIN:
> No, but he's had some very strange adventures. Listen…

CLOSE SHOT: MERLIN. He reads from his letter.

> MERLIN:
> "We were overrun by a troop of French knights but their leader
> said he'd spare our lives if we could answer the riddle - "What is
> it that women desire most?" No-one gave the right answer but
> that evening I met a very ugly old woman and I asked her the
> question and she said "Women are like men, what they desire
> most is their own way" … isn't that a strange story?

CAMERA BACK as he looks up to find LANCELOT and GUINEVERE are
looking at each other and haven't heard a word he has been saying.

> MERLIN:
> It's late, we must go.

LANCELOT stops looking at GUINEVERE, gets up and goes to the door with
MERLIN.

> LANCELOT:
> Good night, my lady.

> GUINEVERE:
> Good night.

The TWO MEN leave and GUINEVERE goes over to the window and looks out.

262.   EXT. COURTYARD. CAMELOT CASTLE. NIGHT.

GUINEVERE stares down and sees LANCELOT and MERLIN come out. MERLIN leaves and LANCELOT looks back up at GUINEVERE.

CLOSE SHOT : GUINEVERE. Her face is at the window. She looks pale and frightened as if she knows something terrible is going to happen.

ACT THREE BREAK

263.   EXT. COURTYARD CAMELOT. DAY.

CARPENTERS and MASONS are still working on the new buildings at Camelot, there is scaffolding everywhere as LANCELOT talks to the aged ARCHITECT.

                    LANCELOT:
          The work's going much too slowly.

                    ARCHITECT:
          You keep changing everything ... first this, then that ... I'm
          doing my best, sire.

                    LANCELOT:
          You'll have to do better than that.

                    ARCHITECT:
          How can I do better than my best?

LANCELOT sees GUINEVERE and joins her.

                    LANCELOT:
          All alone, my lady?

                    GUINEVERE:
          No, Merlin is with me.

As they walk through the building site to the main building, they don't notice the BUILDERS whispering about them.

GUINEVERE:
Merlin is my faithful shadow.

LANCELOT:
That's right and proper.

GUINEVERE:
Why not you? You're my champion.

LANCELOT:
Because when I'm near you I can't control my heart.

GUINEVERE:
(whispering)
You're near me now.

Their hands brush each others.

LANCELOT:
(whispering)
It's dangerous …

GUINEVERE:
(whispering)
Yes …

They are now even closer together. It seems they must kiss. But at that moment MERLIN can be seen striding towards them.

GUINEVERE looks at LANCELOT tenderly.

GUINEVERE:
Perhaps we should be grateful for my shadow.

She abruptly turns and walks over to MERLIN. LANCELOT forces himself to look away.

264.   INT. HALL. CAMELOT. DAY.
         CLOSE SHOT : WALLS.

OLD MERLIN'S VOICE:
I knew it was no use … but I had to try to save Lancelot and Guinevere from themselves … and the horror they could bring down on us all …

Camera back to show MERLIN leaning against a wall as if listening to something. GUINEVERE looks at him in amazement.

> GUINEVERE:
> What's wrong, Merlin?

> MERLIN:
> The walls're whispering, Guinevere, can't you hear them?

> GUINEVERE:
> No, what do they say?

> MERLIN:
> That you're too friendly with Sir Lancelot.

> GUINEVERE:
> Do you listen to such whispers, Merlin?

> MERLIN:
> No, but I've seen you two look at each other …

> GUINEVERE:
> Do you believe we're lovers?!

> MERLIN:
> I don't but others do.

> GUINEVERE:
> I don't care what others think ... I'm the Queen.

> MERLIN:
> That's why you must take special care, Guinevere ... I can't protect you in this matter.

> GUINEVERE:
> If only Arthur would come back..

265.   INT. GUINEVERE'S BEDROOM. CAMELOT. NIGHT.

GUINEVERE is unable to sleep. As she goes to the window to look out, there is a soft tapping at the door.

LANCELOT comes in quietly and looks at her, framed in moonlight.

LANCELOT:
You look so beautiful.

GUINEVERE turns away and looks out of the window at the rocks below.

GUINEVERE:
I should jump ... throw myself on the rocks!

LANCELOT:
Then I'll jump too ... I can't live without you.

They can't resist each other. GUINEVERE turns into his arms. They kiss
passionately and move towards the bed.

266.   INT. ELAINE'S BEDROOM. JOYOUS GARD. NIGHT.

ELAINE, in her nightdress, sits in front of her dressing table, brushing her long
blonde hair.

MAB appears momentarily behind her but ELAINE doesn't see her, as an
IMAGE appears in the dressing table mirror in front of her. It shows
LANCELOT and GUINEVERE, making love on the bed in Camelot.

ELAINE stares at the IMAGE.

ELAINE:
I don't believe it ... Lancelot could never ...

She starts rubbing the mirror compulsively trying to erase the IMAGE.
YOUNG GALAHAD comes in. ELAINE, jumps up and quickly throws a scarf
over the mirror.

YOUNG GALAHAD:
Are you all right, mother?... I heard you talking.

ELAINE:
Talking to who?... It's your imagination ... There's nothing
wrong ... Good night, dear.

YOUNG GALAHAD
Good night, mother.

He leaves. ELAINE turns slowly back to the mirror and fearfully, painfully lifts the scarf off the face of the mirror. The IMAGE of LANCELOT and GUINEVERE making love is still there. ELAINE breaks down sobbing uncontrollably.

267.   INT. HALL. TINTAGEL CASTLE. NIGHT.

CLOSE SHOT: MAB. She smiles in satisfaction.

CAMERA BACK to show she stands by the fire. FRIK and MORGAN LE FEY are playing cards and cheating each other like mad, whilst MORDRED leisurely catches a FLY with his left hand. He puts it up to his ear and listens to it buzzing. He smiles slightly, then crushes the FLY in his hand.

                    MORDRED:
          Auntie, you look extraordinarily pleased with yourself …
          what've you done? … is it terrible? … do tell … I'm sure it's
          perfect …

                    MAB:
          I've made sure Elaine knows Lancelot and Guinevere are lovers.

                    MORDRED:
          How absolutely delicious ... How did you do it?

FRIK puts down his cards

                    FRIK:
          Isn't that a little unworthy of us?

                    MORDRED:
          Unworthy? What does that mean, mother?

                    MORGAN:
          I've forgotten ... what does it mean?

                    MAB:
          Yes, it is unworthy … but I don't like to be told, Frik.

She glares at him and FRIK is thrown across the room to crash against a wall.

MORGAN LE FEY rushes over to help him whilst MORDRED chuckles in delight.

268.   <u>SCENE OMITTED.</u>

269.   <u>INT. ELAINE'S BEDROOM. JOYOUS GUARD. DAY</u>

<u>CLOSE SHOT : DRESSING TABLE</u> MIRROR. The mirror is now normal
only reflecting the room, but it is decorated with thick, black, funeral drapes.

270.   <u>INT. ROYAL APARTMENTS. CAMELOT. DAY.</u>

GUINEVERE is with LANCELOT when MERLIN rushes in.

LANCELOT quickly lets go of GUINEVERE's hands. MERLIN ignores it.

MERLIN:
I warned you, but you didn't listen!

LANCELOT:
What's happened?

271.   <u>EXT. RIVER NEAR CAMELOT. DAY.</u>

The funeral SHIP has come to rest in the reeds by the shore. A circle of
SPECTATORS stand round it, with their heads bowed. They include
LANCELOT, MERLIN and GUINEVERE.

The BODY of LANCELOT's wife, ELAINE, is laid out on a bier on the SHIP.

LANCELOT:
How did she die?

MERLIN:
A broken heart … It was because of you.

LANCELOT is stricken. He suddenly moves away.

GUINEVERE:
Lancelot … where are you going?

LANCELOT:
My son needs me … I'm sorry for everything … Merlin, look
after the Queen while I'm gone.

He turns and looks at GUINEVERE for the last time and then leaves.

CLOSE SHOT: GUINEVERE. Tears are streaming down her face as she knows she will never see LANCELOT again.

> OLD MERLIN'S VOICE:
> In marriage without love, there will be love without marriage ... perhaps I judged them too harshly ... the guilt was mine too... I picked Lancelot after all ... I wish I'd told them that, it might've made it easier ...

271A.   EXT. BEACH. AVALON. DAY

CLOSE SHOT. THE WAVES. The waves roll gently on the shore come in and go out and suggesting the passage of time.

> OLD MERLIN'S VOICE
> And so ... and so ... the years rolled on ... one year merging into the next .. and the next ... and the next ... until ...

272.   SCENE OMITTED.

273.   EXT. CLOISTERS. ABBEY. AVALON. DAY.

Clutching a letter, the FATHER ABBOT runs panting along the cloisters.

274.   INT. NIMUE'S ROOM. ABBEY. AVALON. DAY.

The FATHER ABBOT bursts in on NIMUE.

> FATHER ABBOT:
> Great news ... great news, Nimue ... Arthur's coming home!

> NIMUE:
> Thank God! ... Did he find the Holy Grail?

FATHER ABBOT:
No, but what of that? … he's coming home - Holy Grail or no Holy Grail he should never have left!

NIMUE:
Father, Merlin's free! … He can start living his own life again.

The FATHER ABBOT sits beside her and takes her hand.

FATHER ABBOT:
And it should be with you, my child.

NIMUE:
I know … but what of my faith? ... my vocation?

FATHER ABBOT:
Your true vocation is Merlin, child ... God doesn't want you when you love another ... (he whispers) I shouldn't say this in these hallowed walls, faith is supreme but love is even better.

275.   EXT. PATIO. MONASTERY. AVALON. DAY.

NIMUE utters one word.

NIMUE:
Mab.

MAB appears.

MAB:
I'm here, Nimue.

NIMUE:
You made me a promise years ago … will you keep it?

MAB:
Yes, but what made you change your mind?

NIMUE:
The King's coming home and Merlin is free to be with me … I've discovered all I want is Merlin.

MAB:
Will you live with him in a place I choose?

NIMUE:
If you make me whole again.

MAB:
I have to warn you, Nimue, if you go to this place you can never
leave it.

NIMUE:
Will Merlin come to me there?

MAB:
Yes, he'll come.

NIMUE:
Then do it, Mab.

There is a crack of LIGHTNING and a STORM breaks. NIMUE lifts up her
head to the teeming RAIN. We see she is beautiful again.

276.   EXT. COURTYARD. TINTAGEL CASTLE. DAY.

MAB hurries out of the castle with the fully-grown MORDRED and down the
flight of stone steps to the courtyard where FRIK is waiting with the HORSES.

MAB:
Careful, dear, the steps're very slippery.

MORDRED:
Where're we going?

MAB:
To my land, the land of magic ...

MORDRED:
Can I create monsters?

MAB:
If you wish.

MORDRED:
You're so good to me, Auntie.

MAB:
It won't be all fun and games. Arthur's coming back and
there're things I have to teach you.

MORDRED:
Is Mother coming?

MAB:
No, we don't need her anymore.

MORGAN LE FEY appears at the top of the stone steps.

MORGAN LE FEY:
Mab! Where're you taking my son?

MAB:
It's time …

MORGAN LE FEY:
Without a word, without a by-your-leave.

MAB:
I have to make him ready.

MORGAN LE FEY:
You're not taking him - he's my son, my only son!

MAB:
He's mine!

MORGAN LE FEY:
I gave him love you gave him toys!

MAB:
I gave him life!

MORGAN LE FEY:
If you ever change your faith, it'll be because you no longer think you're God …

FRIK laughs at the joke whilst MORDED smirks at the fact two women are fighting over him.

MORGAN LE FEY:
I'll never let my son go!

As MORGAN LE FEY hurries down the steps, MAB just looks at her coldly. MORGAN LE FEY screams and slips. As she crashes down the steps, FRIK a cry of anguish and rushes to her.

She lays at the bottom of the steps, blood oozing from her head.

MAB watches stonily. MORDRED's only emotion is another of his smiles.

MORDRED:
Hhmm, that was very clever, Auntie.

FRIK cradles MORGAN LE FEY in his arms.

FRIK:
My love, my love.

As MORGAN LE FEY looks up at him, dying, she changes back into the UGLY MORGAN LE FEY, with a cast in her eye.

MORGAN LE FEY:
Frik, my love, am I still beautiful?

FRIK:
Beyond words, my love …

MAB is impatient and changes FRIK back into his former UGLY gnomelike self.

FRIK:
Am I?

MORGAN LE FEY:
Oh yes, beyond words …

They kiss and MORGAN LE FEY dies. FRIK looks at MAB who has been politely helped up on her HORSE by MORDRED.

FRIK:
You killed her!

MAB:
(shrugging)
Perhaps she just slipped … in any case what does it matter? … you're holding us up, Frik, we have a lot to do.

FRIK lowers MORGAN LE FEY's body gently to the ground and stands.

FRIK:
Mab, you evil old crone! May God have mercy on your soul.
He obviously didn't have any on the rest of you!

MAB:
Why is everyone suddenly against me?

FRIK:
Because you've become so monstrous your own shadow won't
keep you company!

MAB:
Frik, I'm leaving you with your misery and pain ... but with no
more magic powers ... Now you'll wander the earth, ugly and
alone like other humans.

MORDRED:
Goodbye, Frik, I'll miss you ... no, I won't.

MORDRED mounts his HORSE and rides away with MAB.

MORDRED:
Why didn't you kill him, Auntie Mab?

MAB:
Because that's what he wanted me to do.

CLOSE SHOT: FRIK and MORGAN LE FEY. FRIK sits on the steps, beside
MORGAN LE FEY'S DEAD BODY and cries.

277.   EXT. COUNTRYSIDE NEAR CAMELOT. DAY.

ARTHUR leads his depleted band of KNIGHTS towards Camelot. GAWAIN
rides beside him. They and their HORSES are weary, their banners droop.

They ride to the top of a rise and there before them on a distant hill is Camelot,
sparkling in the sun.

The KNIGHTS gasp in wonder.

ARTHUR:
Camelot ... it's built ... Lancelot has kept his word.

GAWAIN:
We have to ride in with banners held high, sire!

ARTHUR:
You're right, Gawain ... Lift up your banners and your hearts, men! We're home!

The KNIGHTS cheer, lift up their banners and ride after ARTHUR towards Camelot.

They are too excited to notice a CLOUD has passed over the face of the sun, casting a LONG SHADOW over Camelot.

278.   EXT. COURTYARD. CAMELOT. DAY.

ARTHUR and his KNIGHTS ride in, expecting a warm reception but the courtyard is deserted.

ARTHUR dismounts.

ARTHUR:
Where is everyone?

GAWAIN:
Something's wrong ...

ARTHUR looks round.

279.   INT. THRONE ROOM. CAMELOT. DAY.

ARTHUR strides in with GAWAIN to find GUINEVERE seated on the throne with the NOBLES, SIR BORIS, LORD LOT, SIR HECTOR standing nervously on either side of her. They ALL look uneasily as if expecting a storm to break.

GUINEVERE stands as ARTHUR crosses to her.

ARTHUR:
I didn't expect this kind of homecoming ... what's wrong here? ... Guinevere? ...

GUINEVERE doesn't answer.

ARTHUR:
Lord Lot? ... Sir Hector? ...

Both LORD LOT and SIR HECTOR clear their throats and shuffle uncomfortably.

> ARTHUR:
> Where's Merlin?! ... Where's Lancelot?

> MORDRED:
> I'll tell you ...

MORDRED stands, elegantly poised in the open doorway, sniffing a scented handkerchief. There are a number of NOBLES with him.

> ARTHUR:
> Who the devil're you?

> MORDRED:
> Elegantly put ... "Who the devil?" ... Yes, indeed ... "Who the devil?" ...

He crosses to ARTHUR.

> MORDRED:
> Don't you recognise me?

> ARTHUR:
> No ... should I?

> MORDRED:
> Oh, I'm hurt ... here in the heart, not usually my most vulnerable spot ... I recognise you, Father... I'm your long lost son, Mordred.

The NOBLES react. Some are surprised, others angry at ARTHUR and MORDRED. This is something they didn't want to come out into the open.

ARTHUR turns pale.

> ARTHUR:
> Morgan le Fey is your mother?

> MORDRED:
> Not is, father, was ... she passed over into a better world.

> ARTHUR:
> I'm sorry.

MORDRED:
She sleeps alone at last ... a great loss ... one day she was
laughing, smiling ... the next, gone like a summer breeze... in
the midst of life etc, etc, etc, and so on and so forth ... It's why
I'm here.

ARTHUR:
I don't understand.

MERLIN silently enters the room.

MORDRED:
To protect your interests, Father ... your interests are my
interests ... while you were away on this great spiritual quest to
cleanse your soul ... if you were - how should I put it? - you
were being betrayed.

MERLIN:
Mordred! ... that's enough!

MORDRED:
It isn't! ... come, Merlin, let's speak truth at last ... Father ...

MERLIN:
This isn't the time!

But MORDRED continues remorselessly.

MORDRED'S KNIGHTS:
It is! ... it is!

MORDRED continues despite the OTHERS.

MORDRED:
Father, Lancelot betrayed you with the Queen, or should it be,
the Queen betrayed you with Lancelot? No matter, there's no
point in being pedantic - you were betrayed!

As the KNIGHTS and NOBLES gasp, now it's out in the open, ARTHUR
turns to GUINEVERE.

ARTHUR:
Guinevere?

MERLIN intervenes.

MERLIN:
This is no place to discuss this matter.

MORDRED:
I think it's the perfect place.

MERLIN quickly ushers GUINEVERE and ARTHUR into a side alcove, whilst the NOBLEMEN talk and argue.

ARTHUR:
Guinevere, is it true?

MERLIN:
You're only just back, Arthur ... we must talk calmly and ...

ARTHUR:
Guinevere, is it true?

GUINEVERE:
Yes, it's true.

As ARTHUR reacts in fury, MORDRED appears in the alcove.

MERLIN:
You've no right here, Mordred.

MORDRED:
I've every right here ... we all have .. this isn't a private matter, it concerns us all.

The NOBLES in the background agree.

ARTHUR:
How could you do it, Guinevere? Didn't you think of me?

GUINEVERE:
You left me alone for years, didn't you think of me?! What about my honour, finding out my husband had a child by a woman called Morgan Le Fey?

MORDRED:
Oh dear, oh dear, oh dear ... come, Father, this is becoming distressingly personal. You're forgetting it's a matter of state.

MERLIN:
A matter of state?

MORDRED:
We're talking treason here, aren't we, my lords.

He turns to the tumultuous NOBLEMEN behind him. Some shout "Yes" in agreement. Others look angry and distressed.

ACT FOUR BREAK

280.   <u>INT. HALL OF THE ROUND TABLE. CAMELOT. NIGHT.</u>

The little table has grown, and become HUGE, filling the room, lit by candles. ARTHUR and his other KNIGHTS, including SIR BORIS, LORD LOT, SIR HECTOR, GAWAIN and MERLIN are seated with MORDRED lounging in his chair.

MORDRED:
I'm sorry to cause you pain, Father, but it <u>is</u> treason. When Guinevere betrayed you, she betrayed the crown and the country.

The OTHER KNIGHTS murmur and nod agreement.

ARTHUR:
I don't see it as treason ... she betrayed me and me alone ... that's enough.

SIR BORIS:
No, Mordred is right, sire. You're the King, that makes her adultery, treason.

GAWAIN:
But then we must condemn her to death!

MERLIN:
Do you think we should do that?

LORD LOT:
It's the law.

MERLIN:
It's harsh.

SIR ?:
It's meant to be.

MERLIN:
This is a time when we should temper justice with mercy. Your religion proclaims it. Let he who is not guilty of sin cast the first stone ... I know I've been guilty in my time and I suspect you have been too.

LORD LOT:
I have to confess I've sinned a little.

The OTHERS start to chuckle but MORDRED brings them back to the stark choice.

MORDRED:
So we make excuses for her because she's a Queen.

MERLIN:
No, because she's human.

MORDRED:
No, because she's Arthur's wife! Are we going back to one law for the rulers and one for the ruled. Is that the way it is, Arthur? I thought Camelot was going to be different.

ARTHUR:
It is!

MORDRED:
Then show the world you mean it!

ARTHUR:
Merlin? ... what should I do?

MERLIN looks round the table and senses the majority of the KNIGHTS are with MORDRED in this matter.

MERLIN:
In the end, you must uphold the law.

There is a heavy silence.

ARTHUR:
So be it ... Guinevere will be tried for treason.

As the OTHERS nod in agreement, MERLIN gets up and leaves. MORDRED smiles and claps.

MORDRED:

A splendid decision, both fair and just, eh, Father? ... Now,
let's drink and enjoy ourselves.

ARTHUR looks at him with pure loathing.

ARTHUR:

I want you to leave Camelot!

MORDRED:

But, Father, I only just arrived. I thought we'd reminisce about
old time and play happy families.

ARTHUR:

Stop him talking!

MORDRED:

You can't mean that, Father? I'm your devoted son, the crown
prince, your one and only heir.

ARTHUR:

Get out of my sight!

MORDRED:

Embrace me, Father ...

ARTHUR

Never.

MORDRED

Or I'll take what's rightfully mine.

ARTHUR:

Guards!

TWO GUARDS enter. MORDRED gets up. As the GUARDS move to escort
him out, he pushes them in the chest, without any effort. The GUARDS fly
backwards and smash against the wall.

MORDRED hasn't lost his smile.

MORDRED:

Please don't get up. I know the way out.

He turns at the door.

MORDRED:
I'm sorry, Father, but I'm going to destroy you … and this time your pet wizard won't save you.

He leaves.

DISSOLVE TO:

281.   INT. HALL OF THE ROUND TABLE. LATER THAT NIGHT.

ARTHUR and MERLIN sit alone at the Round Table.

ARTHUR:
I can't let this happen … they'll burn her at the stake.

MERLIN:
It's the only way to save the kingdom.

ARTHUR:
How many of my knights will side with Mordred?

MERLIN:
About half, I think.

ARTHUR:
That many? Why?

MERLIN:
When they found out you had a child by Morgan le Fey some of them felt they'd been betrayed … others have gone over because they want to be on the winning side.

282.   SCENE OMITTED.

282A.   INT. THRONE ROOM. CAMELOT. DAY.

An agitated EXECUTIONER, with traditional black hood, leather apron, noose and axe in his belt, hurries into see ARTHUR and MERLIN. ARTHUR is too disturbed to pay him much attention as he looks out of the balcony window.

EXECUTIONER:
Sire, I've been the Royal Executioner all my working life, but I must protest ... Haven't I given satisfaction? Have I failed in some way? Are you unhappy with my work?

MERLIN:
No, no, everyone's very happy with your work ... I've certainly heard no complaints ... everyone says Iron-Head Gort is the best there is.

EXECUTIONER:
Then why has the time of Queen Guinevere's execution been changed? All executions whether by fire, axe or rope take place at dawn. It's symbolic ... the sun rises up, the condemned man goes down ... it's very beautiful. But it's been decreed the Queen dies at noon ... At noon. It just isn't done.

MERLIN:
(confidentially)
I can't tell you any more at the moment Master Gort but it's a highly secret matter...

EXECUTIONER:
And another thing. Why am I <u>burning</u> her? The penalty for treason is being torn into two pieces by wild horses or hanging

MERLIN shepherds the EXECUTIONER out.

MERLIN:
Do you're best, Master Gort, we trust you'll put on a good show.

283.   EXT. COURTYARD. CAMELOT. DAY.

GUINEVERE, her hands tied behind her, is being taken to the stake through a CROWD. A small CROWD has gathered including MORDRED.

284.   INT. ARTHUR'S ROOM. CAMELOT. DAY.

ARTHUR stands by the window, staring down at the spectacle below, as MERLIN hurries in.

ARTHUR:
I can't bear to watch, the sin was mine not hers.

285.   EXT. COURTYARD. CAMELOT. DAY.

GUINEVERE is being bound to the stake.

All faces are turned towards GUINEVERE at the stake, except MORDRED. He is staring fixedly up at ARTHUR's room and balcony overlooking the courtyard.

CLOSE SHOT: MORDRED. He continues looking up at the room.

CAMERA BACK to show the EXECUTIONER lighting a brand as the ARCHBISHOP intones a prayer.

286.   INT. ARTHUR'S ROOM. CAMELOT. DAY.

MERLIN and ARTHUR watch the execution with increasing anxiety.

287.   <u>EXT. COURTYARD. CAMELOT. DAY.</u>

The EXECUTIONER, with great pomposity and exaggerated gestures, lights
the wood round the stake.

As GUINEVERE closes her eyes, there is a loud commotion and LANCELOT
gallops into the courtyard amid shouts and cries.

Only MORDRED's actions are unexpected. He seems only mildly interested in
LANCELOT's sudden appearance. He still looks up at the King's room.

288.   <u>SCENE OMITTED.</u>

289.   <u>SCENE OMITTED.</u>

290.   INT. ARTHUR'S ROOM. CAMELOT. DAY.

ARTHUR sees what's happening.

                        ARTHUR:
            It's too late! ... she's burning! Merlin!

MERLIN steps forward.

291.   EXT. BALCONY. ARTHUR'S ROOM. DAY.

MERLIN steps out onto the balcony and gestures decisively.

292.   EXT. COURTYARD. CAMELOT. DAY.

CLOSE SHOT: MORDRED. He has seen MERLIN make the magic gestures
and smiles triumphantly.

CAMERA BACK as there is a clap of thunder and a sudden unexpected
CLOUDBURST which douses the flames round the stake.

293.   EXT. BALCONY. ARTHUR'S ROOM. DAY.

MERLIN quickly steps back into ARTHUR's room.

294.   EXT. COURTYARD. CAMELOT. DAY.

In the rain, LANCELOT has cut GUINEVERE free and pulled her onto his
horse. The confusion around him in the rain is so great NO-ONE can stop him
as they gallop away, despite angry shouts.

CLOSE SHOT: MORDRED. He looks very pleased.

294A.   INT. ARTHUR'S ROOM. CAMELOT. DAY.

ARTHUR looks totally relieved.

                        ARTHUR:
            Thank God ...

He realises he has MERLIN to thank too.

> ARTHUR:
> And you, Merlin ...

> MERLIN:
> It had to be done ... I hope nobody saw me.

> ARTHUR:
> It's strange ... when I married Guinevere, I didn't love her ... it was a marriage of state ... but my feelings changed ... I found I did truly love her in the end ... too late.

> MERLIN:
> You've proved it ... this was an act of love, Arthur.

> ARTHUR:
> But it means I'll never see her again.

> MERLIN:
> Never again.

295.   <u>EXT. COUNTRYSIDE. NEAR CAMELOT. DAY.</u>

GUINEVERE and LANCELOT ride past and away into the distance.

> OLD MERLIN'S VOICE:
> And so Lancelot and Guinevere rode out of my story and into legend.

296.   <u>INT. MAIN HALL. CAMELOT. DAY.</u>

The doors of ARTHUR's room bursts open and MORDRED strides in with other NOBLES.

> ARTHUR:
> What's the meaning of this?

> MORDRED:
> You tricked us, Father! You pretended to condemn the Queen to the stake ... then you had her rescued by your damned wizard ... I saw him on the balcony!

The NOBLES murmur darkly.

MORDRED:
You hadn't the courage to set her free yourself!

ARTHUR:
That's true ... I should've done.

MORDRED:
One law for you and another for the rest of us! ...

MORDRED SUPPORTER:
We can't live like that!

MORDRED:
You hear, they can't live like that! ... I call on all true-born
Britons to rally to freedom's flag! Depose this ...

ARTHUR hits him a tremendous backhander that sends him sprawling to the
ground.

MORDRED:
You caught me by surprise, Father.

ARTHUR:
(smiling)
I know how that is.

MORDRED gets up and wipes away a trickle of blood from the corner of his
mouth.

MORDRED:
I give you that free, Father ... for my dear mother's sake ...
Nobles, the time for talking is over! ... those who value right
and justice, follow me ...

He turns and leaves, taking many of the NOBLES with him.

296A.   INT. ROUND TABLE ROOM. CAMELOT. DAY.

The Round Table room is filled with the raised voices and loud crash of armour
against the stone floor, as NOBLES and KNIGHTS assemble for battle. They
are arguing fiercely with ARTHUR. Finally, he gives in and nods in
agreement.

296B.   INT. LOBBY. CAMELOT. NIGHT.

MERLIN comes into the lobby to find the FATHER ABBOT waiting for him.

> FATHER ABBOT:
> I rode all night to get here ... Nimue's gone ... she left you a
> message to say she'll be waiting for you at the door of magic.

> MERLIN:
> You're a liar.

> FATHER ABBOT:
> (shocked)
> Merlin! How can you say that?

> MERLIN:
> You're a liar!

The FATHER ABBOT laughs and turns back into MAB.

> MAB:
> I was glad to see you haven't lost all the skills I taught you.

> MERLIN:
> I've lost none of them ... and it was Frik who taught me.

> MAB:
> Don't mention that ingrate ... Frik has left my employment,
> without a reference.

> MERLIN:
> You mean, he couldn't stand what you've become?

> MAB:
> (shrugging)
> He grew tiresome ... but Nimue _has_ gone and she _does_ want
> you to join her, when you're ready.

MERLIN looks at her.

296C.   INT. ROUND TABLE ROOM. CAMELOT. NIGHT.

ARTHUR sits alone at the Round Table in the deserted hall as MERLIN comes
in.

ARTHUR:
My noblemen don't want you with us against Mordred ... if you come they won't follow me.

MERLIN:
(wryly)
Ah.

ARTHUR:
After all you've done for this country.

MERLIN:
One last lesson for you to learn, Arthur ... gratitude is always in very short supply so don't expect any ...

ARTHUR:
What will you do?

MERLIN:
Close my books, break my wand and retire ... I have a life ... and a chance to live it ...

ARTHUR:
Nimue?

MERLIN:
I'm going to meet her now ... will you be able to deal with Mordred?

ARTHUR:
That beardless whelp! ... it's just one more battle and rights is on your side ...

He gets up and embraces MERLIN.

ARTHUR:
It's been a great adventure ... I just pray I haven't let you down too much.

MERLIN:
I'm proud of you, Arthur.

He starts to leave, then looks back at ARTHUR questioningly.

ARTHUR:
Don't worry about me ... I still have Excalibur.

He unsheaths his SWORD and holds it high.

297.   EXT. COUNTRYSIDE NEAR CAMELOT. DAY.

MERLIN gallops away from Camelot.

298.   EXT. ENCHANTED LAKE. NIGHT.

MERLIN walks along the shore of the lake leading his horse, RUPERT.

> RUPERT:
> Is it much further, Merlin?

> MERLIN:
> No, we're almost there.

> RUPERT:
> It's all a little too much for me now … it's time I was put out to grass.

MERLIN stops and calls.

> MERLIN:
> Nimue! … Nimue!

> NIMUE'S VOICE:
> I'm here, Merlin.

MERLIN peers ahead and sees the entrance to a cave.

299.   INT. ENCHANTED CAVERN. FOREST. DAY.

MERLIN enters the enchanted cavern to find he is in a FOREST.

It looks familiar. In fact, it is the forest around Ambrosia's cottage where he spent his childhood. The only difference is it is brighter, more vivid than the original.

He walks through it in wonder as he sees the ANIMALS he knew as a child.

MERLIN waves to them and walks on to find himself facing Ambrosia's cottage.

Nothing has changed, the FLOWERS, TREES, FENCES, even the WOOD LOGS in the front garden are in place. But there is SMOKE coming out of the cottage chimney.
The door opens and NIMUE comes out. She and MERLIN rush to each other and embrace and kiss.

> NIMUE:
> (pointing at her face)

Look!

Look where we are!

NIMUE grabs MERLIN and gives him a big, bold, passionate kiss right on his mouth.

> MERLIN:
> This is what I've always dreamed of ...

> NIMUE:
> (dragging him seductively into the cottage)

Come

MERLIN stops her.

> MERLIN:
> Lets not forget, it's all Mab.

> NIMUE:
> Forget her! We've wasted too much of our lives together already. Now it's our turn. Isn't it what you always wanted?

MERLIN kisses NIMUE. Passion rises, taking each other's clothes off as they enter the cottage!!!!

300.　　　EXT. BATTLEFIELD. SALISBURY. DAY.

Mist shrouds the Salisbury Plain as ARTHUR'S ARMY with their banners
flying bravely, move forward as if in SLOW MOTION.

ARTHUR leads with GAWAIN and SIR BORIS and the other NOBLES beside
him. They are followed by ARCHERS, PIKEMEN and MEN-AT-ARMS.
Amongst the humble FOOTSOLDIERS, we seek FRIK, festooned with
daggers and clubs, marching determinedly with the OTHERS.

301.　　　EXT. ANOTHER PART OF THE BATTLEFIELD. DAY.

MORDRED, in gleaming black armour and a fantastic helmet, complete with
menacing metal antlers, rides forward at the head of a great ARMY.

They move silently, eerily, forward through the mist which soon swallows
them up.

There is a long haunting silence as we wait for the TWO ARMIES to meet and
the battle to start.

Without warming a HORSE gallops wildly out of the mist, dragging ONE of
ARTHUR's DEAD KNIGHTS, entangled in a torn banner behind him.

We hear the SOUND of savage fighting which grows LOUDER and LOUDER.
A wounded SOLDIER staggers out of the mist, only to be brutally clubbed
down by a KNIGHT on horseback.

CLOSE SHOT: TWO KNIGHTS. They charge at each other through the mist.

CLOSE SHOT: FRIK. He leaps onto a KNIGHT on horseback and repeatedly
stabs him in the back.

CLOSE SHOT: MORDRED. Surrounded by ENEMY SOLDIERS, he cooly
cuts down FOUR of them.

CLOSE SHOT: ARTHUR. EXCALIBUR flashes as he ducks under an Enemy
lance and kills the ENEMY KNIGHT with one blow.

CAMERA BACK to show MORE TROOPS coming out of the mist, brutally fighting and killing. The armoured KNIGHTS are covered with blood as MEN fall, screaming.

302.   <u>INT. GARDEN. COTTAGE. ENCHANTED CAVE. DAY.</u>

NIMUE and MERLIN are laying on the grass in the front garden, in each other's arms under a mellow sun.

> NIMUE:
> This is so beautiful, isn't it?

> MERLIN:
> Yes …

He kisses her but starts as he hears a distant SCREAM.

> NIMUE:
> What is it, Merlin?

> MERLIN:
> I heard a scream.

He hears more CRIES from the distant battlefield.

> NIMUE:
> I didn't hear anything …

> MERLIN:
> It's the sound of battle … Arthur and Mordred.

> NIMUE:
> Oh … but it's nothing to do with us.

> MERLIN:
> No …

<u>CLOSE SHOT: NIMUE and MERLIN.</u> NIMUE is troubled as MERLIN falls silent.

303.   EXT. BATTLEFIELD. SALISBURY. DAY.

ARTHUR has been unhorsed. TWO of MORDRED'S MEN rush him and he cuts them down.

CLOSE SHOT: GAWAIN. He kills a KNIGHT with a sword thrust as MORDRED looms out of the mist.

                              MORDRED:
                    Gawain, what a pleasant surprise.

                              GAWAIN:
                    Stop talking, Mordred, and fight.

                              MORDRED:
          I thought you'd enjoy some light conversation before you die …
          but as you wish …

GAWAIN leaps at him. MORDRED momentarily falters under the onslaught but soon drives GAWAIN back.

Ducking under GAWAIN's sword, MORDRED thrust upwards, piercing GAWAIN's neck.

GAWAIN falls. MORDRED steps forward to finish him off when GAWAIN'S FATHER, LORD LOT comes charging out of the mist, roaring.

MORDRED cuts him down with one terrible blow and LORD LOT falls as OTHER MEN stumble out of the mist, fighting furiously.

CLOSE SHOT: SIR BORIS. As SIR BORIS finds himself overwhelmed, FRIK appears and kills THREE of his ATTACKERS.

ARTHUR joins them.

                              ARTHUR:
                    You all right, Sir Boris?

                              SIR BORIS
                    Just getting my second wind, sire.

                              ARTHUR:
                    Where the devil is Mordred?

                              FRIK:
                    I saw him over there …

He points and ARTHUR rushes off.

304.   <u>INT. GARDEN. COTTAGE. ENCHANTED CAVE. DAY.</u>

<u>CLOSE SHOT: MERLIN.</u> He sits, white-faced and tense for now he is not only hearing but seeing the great battle.

305.   <u>INT. BATTLEFIELD. DAY.</u>

ARTHUR comes out of the mist to be confronted with a smiling MORDRED.

> ARTHUR:
> Mordred.

> MORDRED:
> Hello, Father.

> ARTHUR:
> It's time to settle it.

> MORDRED:
> We agree on that, at least … you know, Father, if you'd lived I don't think we'd've been very happy as a family.

He leaps at ARTHUR and the TWO battle to the death.

ACT FIVE BREAK

The fight is long and bloody. EXCALIBUR delivers blow after blow but MORDRED has the strength and endurance of ten.

Finally ARTHUR makes a supreme effort, EXCALIBUR forces its way past MORDRED's guard and smashes MORDRED's shoulder.

MORDRED falls to his knees. ARTHUR raises EXCALIBUR for the death blow.

> MORDRED:
> (weakly)
> Tut, tut, Father, another sin? … you'd kill your own son?

ARTHUR hesitates for a moment. That is all MORDRED needs, and he stabs ARTHUR.

306. EXT. GARDEN. COTTAGE. ENCHANTED CAVE. DAY.

CLOSE SHOT: MERLIN. He reacts.

307. EXT. BATTLEFIELD. DAY.

ARTHUR staggers and in a fury, turns on MORDRED and runs him through. He falls mortally wounded.

308. INT. MAB'S INNER SANCTUM. ENCHANTED LAND. DAY.

MAB sees MORDRED's fall in a large CRYSTAL and cries out.

MAB:
Mordred!

309. INT. GARDEN. COTTAGE. ENCHANTED CAVE. DAY.

CLOSE SHOT: MERLIN. He suddenly stands.

CAMERA BACK to show NIMUE looking at him.

NIMUE:
What is it, Merlin?

MERLIN:
Arthur's dying … I must go to him.

NIMUE:
You mean leave this place ... and me?

MERLIN:
Yes ... I can't let him die alone.

NIMUE:
You'd let me live alone?

MERLIN:
Come with me then?

NIMUE:

No!

MERLIN:

It's only for a short time. I'll be back ...

NIMUE:

You won't ...

MERLIN is surprised at NIMUE'S attitude not realising she knows he can never come back once he leaves.

MERLIN:

Of course I'll come back. I love it here ... I love you. Why wouldn't I come back? ... I have to do this, Nimue, or I wouldn't be the man you love!

NIMUE suddenly realises the sacrifice she has to make. She puts the palm of her hand up to his face.

NIMUE:
(sadly)
I understand, my love ... I can't keep you here ... go quickly.

MERLIN gently takes her hand from his cheek and he kisses it.

310.   <u>EXT. BATTLEFIELD. DAY.</u>

ARTHUR has sunk to his knees, mortally wounded. He looks up and sees MAB standing over the dying MORDRED.

She moans, too stricken with grief to pay attention to ARTHUR as he drags himself away.

311.   <u>EXT. FOREST. ENCHANTED CAVE. DAY.</u>

MERLIN walks with NIMUE back along the forest path to the entrance to the cave.

MERLIN:

I'll be back very soon.

NIMUE:
I'll be waiting for you ... always.

She smiles wryly at the words because this is where she'll "always" be now.
They kiss.

MERLIN:
Very soon ... I swear ...

MERLIN hurries away but turns back for a moment and waves.

CLOSE SHOT : NIMUE. She is crying as she waves back knowing -
MERLIN can never return to her.

312.   EXT. HILL OVERLOOKING LAKE. DAY.

Clasping EXCALIBUR in his hand, ARTHUR struggles up to the top of the
hill, overlooking a lake.

Then he collapses and slumps down against an old oak tree; he can't go any
further.

ARTHUR:
Merlin ...

313.   SCENE OMITTED.

314.   EXT. ENTRANCE TO ENCHANTED CAVE. DAY.

As MERLIN comes out of the cave, there is a menacing RUMBLE. He turns to
see the cave entrance turn to solid rock. There is no entrance, no cave.

MERLIN instantly realises what a sacrifice NIMUE has made; she is trapped
inside. He can never see her again.

MERLIN:
Nimue! ... Nimue! ...

He searches for the entrance but there is only sheer rock.

OLD MERLIN'S VOICE:
Why didn't she tell me I could never go back? I would never
have left ... she sacrificed herself for me ... I knew I would
never see her again.

He pounds on the rock in despair.

> MERLIN:
> NIMUE! ...

315.   <u>EXT. HILL OVERLOOKING LAKE. DAY.</u>

<u>CLOSE SHOT: ARTHUR.</u> He is slumped against the tree, his head down. He makes no movement, he looks as if he is dead.

But something makes him stir and he looks up.

CAMERA BACK to show MERLIN standing in front of him.

> ARTHUR:
> Ah, old friend ... I knew you'd come ...

MERLIN bends down to him.

> MERLIN:
> How goes the day, Arthur?

> ARTHUR:
> I've seen better ...

He grasps MERLIN's hand urgently.

> ARTHUR:
> Take the sword to the lake ... Mordred mustn't have it ...

MERLIN nods. ARTHUR relaxes his fierce grip on the sword and MERLIN takes it.

MERLIN hesitates, he is reluctant to leave ARTHUR.

ARTHUR tries feebly to push him away.

> ARTHUR:
> Go ... Merlin ... now ...

MERLIN stands up.

> MERLIN:
> Rest easy, son. I won't let you die alone.

> ARTHUR:
> (fiercely)
> You must go!

> MERLIN
> Good times, bad times, you were always more to me
> than a king and a friend, Arthur ...

He gets up.

> MERLIN
> You <u>were</u> the right man to hold Excalibur!

ARTHUR smiles.

MERLIN hurries away down the hill to the lake.

Half way down, he turns back and sees the figure of ARTHUR still
resting against the tree on top of the hill.

But even as MERLIN looks, the FIGURE slowly topples sideways.
ARTHUR is dead.

316.   <u>EXT. LAKE. DAY.</u>

A grief-stricken MERLIN hurries to the water's edge and hurls
EXCALIBUR high into the air.

As the SWORD turns over and over IN SLOW MOTION it "sings" a
melancholy lament.

> MERLIN:
> Take it back Lady! ... You lied to me!

As EXCALIBUR falls, a WOMAN'S HAND, sheathed in a white silk
GLOVE, rises out of the water, catches it, and sinks with it, beneath the
water.

MERLIN collapses and the LADY OF THE LAKE appears beside him.

> LADY OF THE LAKE:
> I didn't lie to you, Merlin. I told you the answer was at
> Joyous Gard.

> MERLIN:
> It's where I found Lancelot ... Ah, it wasn't Lancelot ...

> LADY OF THE LAKE:
> It was the boy ... it was Galahad.

> MERLIN:
> How many mistakes must I make?!

> LADY OF THE LAKE:
> As many as everyone else ... It's human to make
> mistakes, Merlin and part of you is human - the best part.

MERLIN:
Where is Galahad now?

316A.   EXT. DESERT. DAY.

CLOSE SHOT: GALAHAD. Now in his late teens, GALAHAD rides across the desert under a blazing sun. He is in white armour on a WHITE HORSE and carrying a banner of Christ's Cross.

LADY OF THE LAKE'S VOICE:
He's in the Holy Land, on a quest to find Christ's Holy Grail …

DISSOLVE TO:

316B.   EXT. LAKE. DAY.

The LADY OF THE LAKE looks at the stricken MERLIN.

LADY OF THE LAKE:
You'll have to do it yourself … Goodbye, Merlin, we'll never meet again.

MERLIN:
Why?

LADY OF THE LAKE:
My time is past … My sister Mab was right about one thing … when we're forgotten, we cease to exist …

She vanishes back into the lake.

317.   SCENE OMITTED.

318.   EXT. BATTLEFIELD. DAY.

Amid the clinging mist MAB tries to revive the dying MORDRED but cannot.

MAB:
I can't save you … don't die, Morded.

MORDRED:
Die, dear Auntie Mab? … that's the last thing I shall do.

He smiles and dies.

MAB lets out a great silent howl. There is an almighty CLAP OF THUNDER.

MAB:
I swear I'll make the whole world pay!

319.   EXT. ANOTHER PART OF THE BATTLEFIELD. DAY.

The remains of ARTHUR'S ARMY, including SIR BORIS, GAWAIN and
FRIK are grouped around a gnarled and broken tree. They are dispirited and do
not look in any condition to continue the battle.

They hardly react as MERLIN rides up and dismounts. He sees FRIK.

MERLIN:
Frik, what're you doing here?

FRIK:
Betraying my principals. I've always believed it's better to be a
coward for a second than dead for a lifetime. But here I am
fighting - and fighting on the side of right what's worse!

MERLIN:
And Mab?

FRIK:
I gave in my notice … If you're going after her you'll need help.

MERLIN:
All I can get, my friend.

320.   SCENE OMITTED.

321.   INT. GREAT HALL. CAMELOT. DAY.

MERLIN followed by FRIK walking purposely for the great door to the Round
Table room. Without breaking stride he gestures and they swing open for him.

321A.   INT. ROUND TABLE ROOM. CAMELOT. DAY.

MERLIN strides in with FRIK to find MAB seated triumphantly at the empty
Round Table.

                    MERLIN:
          I knew you'd be here, Mab.

                    MAB:
          So you've come to see my final triumph.

                    MERLIN:
          No, I've come to see your final defeat.

                    MAB:
          You were always a dreamer … You've lost Arthur, the battle,
          and your one true love …

                    MERLIN:
          The battle isn't over.

                    MAB:
          You can't win.

FRIK whispers to MERLIN.

                    FRIK:
          She's weakened herself … she's vulnerable.

                    MERLIN:
          I know now what we have to do …

As he whispers instructions to FRIK, MAB gets up.

                    MAB:
          Why're you talking to that traitor?

                    FRIK:
          After all my years of faithful service; that's very harsh, Madam.

                    MAB:
          Not as harsh as I'm going to be.

                    FRIK:
          Sorry, can't stay.

He darts back into the Great Hall.

> MAB:
> Mordred's dead.

> MERLIN:
> Ah ... So the battle is just between you and me, Mab...

MAB nods in agreement and the Round Table splits violently as the two parts are flung against opposite walls.

MAB looks at MERLIN and creates a sudden tremendous wind that blows him off his feet and into the air and smashes him against the wall.

ACT SIX BREAK

MERLIN is spreadeagled and half-way up the wall. He gestures and the magical wind stops blowing and MERLIN lands gently on his feet.

> MAB:
> I'll show you how weak I am.

A rain of LETHAL SPEARS hurtle straight at him. He gestures, creates a LARGE SHIELD and ALL the SPEARS embed themselves in it.

Through it all, MERLIN never retaliates. He just lets MAB expend her waning powers.

MAB advances on MERLIN who retreats.

> MAB:
> I might be weaker, Merlin, but I can still deal with these poor humans ... Are you going to use your swords, clubs, pikes and axes on me?

> MERLIN:
> No, we're going to forget you, Mab.

MAB's next move is to throw a swirling burst of fire at him. MERLIN gestures diverting the swirling FIREBALL so it hits the wall behind him. MAB throws ANOTHER and ANOTHER. Each one is diverted by MERLIN so they hit the wall behind him. The doors are smashed down so we see the Great Hall.

MERLIN signals to FRIK as GAWAIN and the TROOPS packed in the Great Hall, simply turn their backs on MAB.

MAB:
Merlin, what're you doing?

MERLIN:
You can't fight us or frighten us … you're just not important
enough anymore … We forget you, Queen Mab … go join your
sister in the lake and be forgotten.

He turns his back on MAB who screams in rage and fear. She stares at
MERLIN and the OTHERS, trying to invoke magic but nothing happens.

Neither the ARMY nor MERLIN move.

MAB:
Look at me! Look at me! …

But the TROOPS don't turn round, instead they just begin to walk away out of
the far end of the Great Hall.

MAB:
Frik! …

The TROOPS keep walking away so they don't see that MAB is beginning to
FADE.

MERLIN too begins to move away.

MAB:
(frightened)
Merlin! …

CLOSE SHOT: MERLIN. He doesn't react to her cries.
MAB'S VOICE:
Don't forget me, Merlin … you know I love you … as a
son …

CLOSE SHOT: MAB. She has already FADED AWAY.
MAB:
I love you … Merlin … Merlin …

She DISAPPEARS forever.

OLD MERLIN'S VOICE:
Perhaps she did, despite everything … whether she did nor not,
it was the end of her… Galahad returned …

DISSOLVE TO:

321A.   EXT. COUNTRYSIDE. DAY.

GALAHAD rides through the winter landscape, carrying the Holy Grail, a silver cup that shines with a strange light.

As he passes bare trees, barren fields and frozen streams, they change. The TREES sprout leaves, the STREAMS melt and the FIELDS become full of golden wheat and CHILDREN can be seen laughing and playing.

                    OLD MERLIN'S VOICE:
          And he brought with him the Holy Grail ... and Spring, and the
          land became fertile again and the cycle of darkness and death
          ended, and so does my story ...

                         DISSOLVE TO:

322.   SCENE OMITTED.

323.   SCENE OMITTED.

324.   SCENE OMITTED.

325.   SCENE OMITTED.

326.   EXT. COUNTRY FAIR. DAY.

CLOSE SHOT: OLD MERLIN. This is exactly the SAME SHOT of the traditional old white-bearded cone-hatted OLD MERLIN we started with.

CAMERA BACK to show OLD MERLIN has been telling the story to an AUDIENCE who sit in a circle around him in the middle of a country fair.

OLD MERLIN sits in front of a banner which proclaims "MERLIN - MASTER STORYTELLER"

A YOUNG GIRL asks a question.

YOUNG GIRL:
Master Merlin, did you ever find Nimue?

OLD MERLIN:
(sadly)
No, I never found Nimue or even the cave again.

The YOUNG GIRL looks sad.

MAN
What about the magic, can you still do magic?

OLD MERLIN:
No, I've got out of the habit and nobody believes in it
anymore …

The AUDIENCE starts to stand up.

OLD MERLIN:
If my story entertained or enchanted, you may show your
appreciation in any way you think fit … but particularly with
money.

He points to a collection box on a table nearby.

As SOME of the AUDIENCE put money into it, OLD MERLIN gets up
creakily. As he stretches his arms and cracks his back, he notices ONE of the
AUDIENCE hasn't moved.

OLD MERLIN:
It's all over, friend, there is no more.

The MAN looks up. It is FRIK.

FRIK:
That's not the way I remember it, Merlin.

OLD MERLIN recognises the voice and comes closer and peers. It is FRIK
though older and white-haired.

OLD MERLIN:
Frik, is it you?

FRIK:
Yes, it's me …

They embrace.

FRIK:
I must say, you tell a good tale but you did embroider it a little … I mean, all that business with …

OLD MERLIN:
Dramatic licence … that's what they like. I don't think they'd believe it if I told them how it really was …

They go over to the collection box.

OLD MERLIN:
And how are you doing in this world, Frik?

FRIK:
Well … there's always a need for the perfect gentleman's gentleman, and I was, and I always will be, one of the best.

OLD MERLIN takes the small amount of money out of the box.

OLD MERLIN:
Meagre pickings, Frik, meagre pickings.

FRIK:
Then it's true. You don't do any magic anymore.

OLD MERLIN:
That's right, but the real reason is it brings back too many sad memories.

FRIK:
I know about them … but that's why I'm here … come with me …

FRIK leads OLD MERLIN behind one of the tents where a VERY OLD HORSE is tethered. OLD MERLIN peers at it.

OLD MERLIN:
It can't be … it is … Sir Rupert.

RUPERT neighs in recognition as OLD MERLIN and FRIK come up to him.

FRIK:
I found him grazing in a field and we got to reminiscing.

OLD MERLIN strokes RUPERT's mane.

OLD MERLIN:
Shouldn't you be dead by now?

RUPERT:
No, no, there's a little magic in me too, Merlin.

FRIK:
Oh yes, I almost forgot ... Nimue ...

OLD MERLIN:
What about her?

FRIK:
(casually)
Oh, she was asking about you when I saw her last month.

OLD MERLIN stares at him in astonishment.

OLD MERLIN:
Nimue?

FRIK:
Yes, Nimue.

FRIK and RUPERT enjoy a horse-laugh at OLD MERLIN's look.

OLD MERLIN:
I don't understand ... what happened?

FRIK:
Sometime after Mab disappeared, her spells began to lose their
power ... and Nimue found herself free ... she's been searching
for you ever since.

OLD MERLIN:
(eagerly)
Where is she, Frik?

FRIK:
Sir Rupert knows.

The HORSE nods his head vigorously.

OLD MERLIN shakes FRIK's hand.

> OLD MERLIN:
> Thank you for everything.

> FRIK:
> Don't thank me ... I just love happy endings.

327.   EXT. FOREST. DAY.

OLD MERLIN finds himself riding through the forest he knew when he was growing up. But it is the real one this time, not the illusionary one Mab created for him in the cave.

OLD MERLIN rides into the clearing with Ambrosia's cottage. There is more ivy round the walls, and the thatched roof is a little bedraggled. But it is Ambrosia's cottage and there is smoke coming from the chimney.

As OLD MERLIN dismounts, the cottage door opens and OLD NIMUE comes flying out to greet him. Her hair is grey and she is much older but still beautiful.

They rush to each other and embrace.

> OLD NIMUE:
> Merlin ...

> OLD MERLIN:
> My dearest ...

They kiss.

> OLD NIMUE:
> Frik found you.

> OLD MERLIN:
> I never believed I'd ever see you again ... so many years lost...

They walk towards the cottage.

> OLD NIMUE:
> You've grown older.

OLD MERLIN:
You too.

OLD NIMUE:
Does it matter?

OLD MERLIN:
Not now … but …

OLD NIMUE:
But?

OLD MERLIN:
I think I still have one trick left.

He concentrates hard for a moment and gestures.

He and NIMUE become YOUNG again. NIMUE laughs in delight and they kiss.

MERLIN:
There's no more … that's the end of magic.

They go into the cottage together, banging the door shut behind them.

FADE OUT

THE END

STILLS

Above: On the set of *Merlin* in Wales, blessed by fine Fall weather.

MERLIN
Sam Neill

204

NIMUE
Isabella Rossellini

FRIK
Martin Short

MAB

Miranda Richardson

VORTIGERN
Rutger Hauer

KING CONSTANT
John Gielgud

MORGAN LE FEY
Helena Bonham Carter

Above: Young lovers Nimue *(Agnieszka Koson)* and Merlin *(Daniel Brocklebank)*.
Below: Have Steadicam, will travel (on the beach in Wales).

Above: Merlin *(Sam Neill).*

Below: On location in Wales: from right, Steve Barron (director), Sam Neill, Gareth Tandy (first assistant director), and Sergei Kozlov (director of photography). Kozlov also served as director of photography on *The Odyssey,* the 1997 Hallmark Entertainment/NBC miniseries.

Above: Director Steve Barron, on the set in Wales.
Below: Merlin *(Neill)* with Excalibur.

Above: Merlin *(Neill)* and Arthur *(Paul Curran)*.
Below: Merlin *(Neill)* and Nimue *(Isabella Rossellini)*.

Above: Nimue *(Rossellini).*

Above: Frik *(Martin Short)* and Mab *(Miranda Richardson)* up to no good.
Below: Mab *(Richardson)* casting a spell.

Above: Frik *(Short)* as Erroll *(Flynn),* one of his many incarnations.
Below: Frik *(Short)* and Morgan Le Fey *(Helena Bonham Carter)* flirt and plot, plot and flirt.

Above: Executive Producer Robert Halmi, Sr., with Sam Neill.
Below: Let the battle begin (near Pinewood).

Above: Merlin *(Neill)* with Excalibur on the battlefield.

Above: Merlin *(Neill)* with the dying Arthur *(Curran).*

Above: Old Merlin *(Neill, after four hours in hair and make-up).*

Above: Steve Barron, the director, on the set near Pinewood.

A CONVERSATION WITH

STEVE BARRON

Steve Barron *(The Adventures of Pinocchio, Teenage Mutant Ninja Turtles)* directs *Merlin*, the magical adventure story, for NBC and Hallmark Entertainment. He was interviewed on the *Merlin* set at London's Pinewood Studios.

QUESTION: *What's your goal with this* Merlin?

STEVE BARRON: I want to maintain feature-picture quality through what is, in effect, *two* feature films, *two* 90-minute films. For the viewer, I want it to be real and enchanting and entertaining. And innovative. I want to do something that excites people and that keeps them enthralled captivated.

What's innovative about this production?

Well, apart from theatrical releases like *Jurassic Park* or *Dragonheart*, you won't have seen the level of creatures that we're going to create with computer graphics. We've got almost 500 effects shots in this picture; most features that use effects have maybe 150.

And then we're using some tools and gadgets that just haven't been used in prime time television, like the Snorkel camera, which has a special mirror at the end of the lens that allows the camera to get into places that a camera can't usually get into.

But this *Merlin* isn't all technical razzmatazz. We have a great concept, a great story, a great myth, fabulous characters. The script is beautifully written, really engaging, with immense wit and charm. All the effects will just enhance what we already have.

I should also point out that with such a stunning cast there will seldom be a moment when the audience isn't being blown away by startling special effects or some brilliant acting—or both! We've got the whole enchilada!

How was this cast assembled?

It's interesting. In any project, you have your number one dream actor for each character, and your number two, and sometimes your number twenty-two! And often it gets down to number twenty-two!

But with *Merlin,* we've been blessed, because we've landed our number one candidate in virtually every case.

For any director, this would be very exciting. Not only do we have a host of great actors, each one is precisely right for his or her role.

How are you dealing with the pressure to direct, as you say, the equivalent of two feature films back-to-back, in just fourteen weeks?

It's tough, no denying that. The bigger it gets, the tougher it gets, the more microcosmic environments you have to deal with. The bigger it is, the harder it is, just to hold it all together.

But on the plus side, you can't help but get a major adrenaline rush from knowing that you just have to do it, you just have to get in there and race. And that fast pace is translating onto the screen. This is the first time I've ever shot feature quality at this pace before and I must say, I now understand why Steven Spielberg works this way. Nothing sags in the middle. You don't get shots that are at a different, slower rhythm. Spielberg feels that, at the end of the day, that *drive* translates onto the screen. He's right. If nothing else, this *Merlin* has *energy!*

Could we talk about some of the actors? Sam Neill . . .

Merlin could be played any number of ways. We decided when writing this we wouldn't go the Nicol Williamson route, the *Excalibur* nutty-professor, conical-hat route. That works if it's just a short bit; otherwise, it's 'enough-already.'

We decided that for this longer, more cerebral *Merlin,* the central character had to have an inner calm, an inner strength. In this mad world where kings are entirely insane, and where he's trying to bring peace to England and the right person to the throne, Merlin had to be the calm in the center of the storm, he had to be the point of stability around which all the madness was flowing. And within that stable sphere, he uses his magic powers sparingly, only when and where he has to use them. He never uses them frivolously.

Sam Neill is the actor who can capture that calm, that sense of judiciousness.

Isabella Rossellini . . .

She is absolutely gorgeous, and she's a lovely person—and those qualities radiate on the screen. You can't help but love her. Nimue is a hugely sympathetic character, and the audience is going to fall in love with Isabella playing her.

Miranda Richardson . . .

I've been a fan of hers for years. She's a fantastic actress.

You have to ask yourself, who would be your number one choice to play Mab? My God, it's a no-brainer. She was always on top of the list. It's just fate that we got her.

Helena Bonham Carter . . .

She's proved time and time again that she's a superb actress. Have you seen *Wings of the Dove*? She's brilliant in that . . . and she's been brilliant in virtually everything she's ever done.

We felt this role would be really interesting for her, because it's a little bit different. Her character, Morgan, has two distinct sides to her. There's a really dark, psychotic side—Helena's never really played that before—and a lighter side, which she's used to playing. We're excited that she can get hold of something that's a little different for her.

Martin Short . . .

I've always found him hysterical, a very funny actor. His timing is brilliant. When you think of *Father of the Bride* and some of the other films he's been in, you just have to marvel at his talent. He's part of that Canadian school of comedy—and they're a very funny clan. Something's going on in

Canada that breeds these comedians—maybe it's the water, or the cold, or something!

What would you say to the audience that's going to be watching Merlin*?*

I'd say this is going to be, cinematically, a vast—even epic—production, which is rare in television. It's so nice to be able to have the resources to create something that really has a sense of scale to it. People are also going to see tremendous performances by several great actors.

Merlin is a great showpiece, and it's all based on a treasure-trove of mythology that's lived a thousand years. Generations upon generations have listened to these myths, and passed them on. To say they've stood the test of time would be a great understatement!

This *Merlin* is a delectable cocktail of succulent goodies!

A CONVERSATION WITH

SAM NEILL AND ISABELLA ROSSELLINI

Sam Neill *(Jurassic Park)* plays the title character and Isabella Rossellini *(The Odyssey)* is Nimue, the woman he loves, in *Merlin*. They were interviewed on a *Merlin* set, in a forest near Pinewood Studios.

QUESTION: *How much did you know about your character, and about the whole Merlin mythology, prior to joining this cast?*

SAM NEILL: Merlin's a rather sketchy character, actually. There were many people who were Merlin, and there was no one who was Merlin. He's clearly based on several historical figures about whom we know very little.

It's pretty clear, too, that there was an early king named Arthur. But we know very little about him. What survives is a series of legends, all of which describe him and his times quite differently.

My research is based primarily on Mallory, which I read at university. I've also studied Druidism—one of the things that we know about Merlin is that he was the last of the Druids. He was the last great Druid priest. I find all that very interesting.

ISABELLA ROSSELLINI: I didn't really know much about the Merlin legend. I went to school in Italy and France, so the only part of the legend I knew about was the Crusades, and a little bit about the Holy Grail.

What I loved about the script is that it seemed like a fairy tale. It was so adventurous. That's what really captured me. There were good people and there were bad people, and I was happy to be playing a good person.

But when I delved into the literature I discovered that my character, Nimue, could often be a dark character. Obviously, she's the one Merlin loves—but she's also the one who enchants Merlin and takes him away from his duty. So in a way the story's about the struggle between the warrior who has the responsibility of searching for the right person to rule the country, versus the man who tries to connect with the person he loves.

Finally, of course, Nimue is a positive character. But she does take Merlin away from Arthur, away from his responsibilities.

Tell us about the Merlin/Nimue relationship . . .

IR: They meet first when they're very young, and it's love at first sight. It's interesting that in the literature you read again and again about these men who were great warriors—and yet, when they encountered a woman, they didn't even talk to her, because she was surrounded by ladies-in-waiting. These men would fall completely, irrationally, in love without even *meeting* the object of their desire—and then ruin their lives in pursuit of love!

On one level, they were masters of the universe; on another level, they were slaves to love. They were tormented by love.

Merlin and Nimue are quite different people. Nimue's of the new religion; Merlin isn't, really. Also, Merlin's a fighter; he only turns to magic when he's exhausted all other sources of strength. Nimue's like a female Gandhi. She certainly doesn't believe in revenge—which is what drives Merlin. She's a product of the new religion; she's ruled by compassion, and by her heart.

SN: Obviously, Merlin's relationship with Nimue is how Merlin's character is 'humanized' throughout our story.

Merlin is, after all, half-wizard, half-human. How better to show his 'human' side than to have him fall in love with a beautiful woman, a woman who later becomes hideously scarred?

Having Nimue in the piece is a great dramatic device that allows the audience to really identify with—and sympathize with—Merlin. She helps make Merlin much more than just a comic-book hero.

What's it been like, working with director Steve Barron?

SN: He's very interested in the humanity of his characters, which is the quality I value most in a director.

The other priceless asset he brings to *Merlin* is a kind of MTV sensibility. He understands the grammar and technique of contemporary filmmaking completely. And in a film in which there's such an enormous number of special effects, it's awfully important that the director be a technologist, as well as an artist.

It also helps, of course, that he's worked extensively with the folks at the Jim Henson Creature Shop. He can speak in shorthand with them, and that's important when you're trying to meet the tough delivery deadlines we have to meet on *Merlin,* to have it ready for broadcast just a few months from now.

Isabella, you were also in last year's The Odyssey. *Did you think it was going to do as well as it did?*

IR: Honestly, I was surprised it did so spectacularly well.

I mean, we knew when we were making it that it was a good film. You could feel that, somehow. But *The Odyssey* was based on a book, a classic, and I was afraid some people would criticize us for tampering with it. But nobody did, and the audience loved it.

I'm not as concerned about *Merlin.* As Sam pointed out, there are very few—if any—*facts* that get in the way of telling this great story. The writers have fleshed out some fabulous characters, and put them in interesting situations.

SN: Let's not forget, there's a very good reason the saga of *The Odyssey* survived so many centuries, and there's a very good reason why the whole Merlin mythology is alive and thriving fifteen hundred years after the Dark Ages.

They're *both* great stories, about extraordinary people living in extraordinary times.

What do you think the audience is for Merlin?

SN: I think the potential audience is vast: men and women, all ages and backgrounds. There's literally something for everyone. Much more than 'something,' actually.

There's a treasure-trove of great material. And I think audiences today are hungry for this kind of raw and powerful story-telling.

IR: I think what's so great about *Merlin* is that I have a four-year-old, and he's going to love this; he'll be entranced by the dragons and the special effects and the magic. And adults are going to embrace it because this legend is known all around the world; people love this story and these characters, and this film explores and enriches all that.

I really believe there's something in it for everybody. It's a family film, and I think this kind of material is badly needed nowadays—there's so little of high quality out there.

And yet there's nothing watered-down or saccharin about this. Actually, it's quite gritty in a lot of places. But ultimately it's life-affirming. The forces of good *do* triumph, and in a time of muddled morality, it brings tears to your eyes when that happens.

MIRANDA RICHARDSON

Miranda Richardson *(The Crying Game)* plays Mab, the evil sorceress, in the Hallmark Entertainment miniseries, *Merlin*. Mab creates Merlin as an ally in her quest to prevent "the new ways" (specifically, Christianity) from triumphing in seventh-century England. She was interviewed on the *Merlin* set, at London's Pinewood Studios.

QUESTION: *Why were you attracted to this project?*

MIRANDA RICHARDSON: Because when I'm playing Mab I can draw on lots of different things. She's multi-dimensional. She's not totally wicked. She actually starts off as quite a beneficent character, then she becomes much darker, and obsessed. In the end, she uses her power to achieve very negative ends, I'm afraid to say.

The challenge is to achieve a balance between exercising great restraint—which Mab does when she's saving her energy, for example—and pulling out all the stops, which is what happens when she's wreaking total havoc.

For an actor, it's all quite liberating. You can let your imagination run riot!

How do you describe Mab's mission?

She's trying to preserve and protect the Old Ways, which is basically paganism. That's what she sets out to do, by any means possible. And then it all just goes wrong. For example, she creates this fabulous wizard, Merlin. But Merlin has his own ideas about how to do things. He doesn't want the powers that she's bestowed upon him. The human side of him wins out, in a way. He's developed a sense of what's right and what's wrong. He's *emotional*, as well as being a great warrior. He even falls in love, for Heaven's sake!

The ultimate tragedy, of course, is that toward the end she lays waste to everything and everybody around her—and yet she can see that it's really not getting her anywhere, that ultimately it's self-destructive. The Old Ways can't win, won't win. No matter what she does, the old paganism is destined for defeat.

How would you describe her relationship with Frik, played by Martin Short?

He's her lackey, really—a complete sycophant. It's a master/slave relationship, and Mab's at her most playful—and her most sadistic—when she's with him. Frik's a marvelous character and Martin Short's having a ball playing him, in all his many incarnations.

This is an amazing sound that's coming out of your throat. How are you doing it?

What I'm trying to do is not so much a *voice*, as utter a kind of underground sound. Early on in the piece it probably is more vocal, but as her character gets darker and darker, Mab lapses into a whisper that gets darker and darker.

I wanted there to be a kind of magic quality to it, so that somebody two hundred yards away could hear it, as could somebody standing right next to Mab. It's a very inner voice. I didn't want my face to move much at all, I wanted the sound to appear to come from some other place, really—not necessarily from my mouth.

And what glorious costumes and hair you have! . . .

The costume says a lot, really. It's encrusted with gemstones—and Mab gets a lot of energy from rocks and gems. She literally unleashes the energy from rocks and gems. And you'll notice many of them are blood red—quite appropriate!

As for the hair, I think Mab just likes her hair like this—long, glamorous, piled on high. I don't think there's any rhyme or reason for its being like this. Somehow it just seems right. It's warrior-like, in a way, and it's good that it's long—it can trail behind you when you're flying through the air!

This whole thing is so extreme, anything goes . . .

What's it like, working with Sam Neill as Merlin?

Sam's great. It's like being with a laid-back captain of a jumbo jet. You know, you just sit back and you're totally confident someone's going to serve you a great meal with lovely wine, and that everything's going to be just fine, thank you very much.

I love the way Sam's playing Merlin. He's very humane. He doesn't have an extreme look. This isn't the Merlin we're used to from films like *Camelot*.

We see Merlin grow up, and we see him develop into a rather Jesus-like character. Sam makes him vulnerable, too. Merlin makes mistakes. He goes through life and some things work out, and some things don't work out. He enjoys success, he experiences failure. He's *believable*.

What's the appeal of this whole Merlin legend to you?

I'm sure we'd all like to believe that there's some secret hope for the country. In times of great strife—and God knows, it's happening all over the world—we'd like to believe that someone will rise up and say, 'This is what we have to do to make things better.'

I think the yearning for that saviour, if you will, is very deep-seated, very entrenched.

Also, the Merlin saga is peopled with fabulous heroes and dastardly villains, and it's set in a time which is mysterious. Not for nothing is it called the Dark Ages!

BIOGRAPHIES

SAM NEILL (Merlin) has, from his first film, been recognized as an actor of extraordinary depth and range. A graduate of Canterbury University, the New Zealand-raised Neill began his film career in 1978, starring in Roger Donaldson's *Sleeping Dogs*. The following year, he played opposite Judy Davis in the acclaimed Australian feature *My Brilliant Career*. Since then, he has starred in dozens of films, including *Plenty* (1985), *A Cry in the Dark* (1988, opposite Meryl Streep), *Dead Calm* (1989, opposite Nicole Kidman), *The Hunt for Red October* (1990) and *Sirens* (1994). Fans most often recognize Neill from his starring roles in a pair of 1993 films, Steven Spielberg's *Jurassic Park* and the critically acclaimed *The Piano* (opposite Holly Hunter and Harvey Keitel). Other recent films include *Country Life* (1995), *Restoration* (1995), *Children of the Revolution* (1997, again opposite Judy Davis) and *Event Horizon* (1997, with Laurence Fishburne). He will also be seen in *The Horse Whisperer*, starring opposite Robert Redford and Kristin Scott Thomas.

Neill's television work includes the TV movies *The Blood of Others*, *Fever*, *One Against the Wind* (Hallmark Hall of Fame, Golden Globe nomination) and *Snow White: A Tale of Terror* (with Sigourney Weaver) as well as the miniseries *Kane and Abel*, *Amerika*, *Family Pictures* and Hallmark Entertainment's *In Cold Blood*. His voice was also heard in an episode of *The Simpsons*.

HELENA BONHAM CARTER (Morgan Le Fey) has, from her debut as the teenage Queen of England in 1985's *Lady Jane*, bewitched audiences with her remarkable talent and a beauty that seems to be drawn from an Edwardian painting. *Time* magazine's Richard Corliss has called her "our modern antique goddess."

A native of London, Bonham Carter is the great-granddaughter of H. H. Asquith, who served as England's Prime Minister from 1908 to 1916. Her father was a Harvard-educated banker, and her mother a psychotherapist. Bonham Carter was accepted at Cambridge University, but after landing the lead in *Lady Jane* at age eighteen, decided to pursue acting as a career. Her next film (and the first of four she has made based on E.M. Forster novels), *A Room with a View,* first brought her to the attention of American audiences. She has also starred in *The Vision* (1987), *Francesco* (1989), Kenneth Branagh's *Hamlet* (1990), *Howard's End* (1992), *Mary Shelley's Frankenstein* (1994), *Mighty Aphrodite* (1995) and *Twelfth Night* (1996).

Bonham Carter has recently garnered rave reviews for two new films, *Keep the Aspidistra Flying* (based on a George Orwell work) and *The Wings of the Dove* (based on a Henry James novel). For American television, Bonham Carter starred as Marina Oswald, wife of Kennedy assassin Lee Harvey Oswald, in the NBC movie *Fatal Deception* (1993).

JOHN GIELGUD (King Constant) is universally recognized as one of the greatest interpreters of Shakespeare ever. Gielgud was born April 14, 1904, and is the great-nephew of the celebrated nineteenth-century British actress Ellen Terry. His own career began in 1921 when, at the age of seventeen, he appeared in *Henry V* at London's Old Vic. His *Hamlet* at the Old Vic has become the stuff of theatrical legend. Throughout the 1930s, Gielgud not only played Shakespeare, but also starred in Oscar Wilde's *The Importance of Being Earnest,* J.B. Priestley's *The Good Companions,* George Bernard Shaw's *Arms and the Man* and Chekhov's *The Seagull.*

After repeated success in myriad Shakespeare roles at Stratford-upon-Avon, Gielgud turned his sights to the works of more modern dramatists, including Noel Coward's *Nude with a Violin,* Graham Greene's *The Potting Shed,* Edward Albee's *Tiny Alice,* Alan Bennett's *Forty Years On,* Harold Pinter's *No Man's Land* and David Storey's *Home.*

Gielgud's screen career began in 1924 with *Who is that Man?* He has since appeared in more than sixty feature and television films, including *Around the World in 80 Days, Becket* (Academy Award nomination), *The Shoes of the Fisherman, The Charge of the Light Brigade, Oh! What a Lovely War, Joseph Andrews, Chariots of Fire, The Elephant Man, Gandhi, Plenty, Shining Through, First Knight, The Portrait of a Lady* and *Prospero's Books.* He received an Academy Award as Best Supporting Actor for *Arthur.*

Gielgud's many television projects include *Brideshead Revisited, War and Remembrance, Scarlett* and *Gulliver's Travels.*

RUTGER HAUER (Lord Vortigern) has starred in over fifty films and continues to create a broad range of memorable characters. As the intelligent yet brutal replicant in Ridley Scott's *Blade Runner,* the homeless man in Ermanno Olmi's *The Legend of the Holy Drinker,* the brave underground fighter in *Soldier of Orange,* or the dark-hearted menace in *The Hitcher*, the Dutch-born Hauer is an actor who reveals both beauty and tragedy in all his performances.

In 1973, Hauer burst on the European film scene in Paul Verhoeven's *Turkish Delight*. The film received an Academy Award nomination for Best Foreign Language Film. In 1980, American audiences were introduced to Hauer when he starred opposite Sylvester Stallone in the action-adventure film *Nighthawks*. The following year he received critical acclaim for his role as a deadly but tragically touching android in *Blade Runner*. The film has become a science fiction classic, and is the youngest film ever added to the National Film Archives maintained by the Library of Congress. In 1982, Hauer first appeared on American television as SS architect Albert Speer in *Inside the Third Reich*.

Hauer's body of work is appreciated by action fans as well as devotees of art-house films. In 1985, he starred opposite Michelle Pfeiffer in *Ladyhawke*, and his performance in *The Legend of the Holy Drinker* earned him the Best Actor Award at the Seattle Film Festival.

Hauer also received a Golden Globe for his role as a compassionate Russian officer in the miniseries *Escape from Sobibor*. Other notable film credits include *Blind Fury*, *A Breed Apart*, *Surviving the Game*, *Mariette in Ecstacy*, *Amelia* (opposite Diane Keaton) and *Fatherland* (Golden Globe nomination).

JAMES EARL JONES (The Mountain King) was born on January 17, 1931 in Tate County, Mississippi. While young, he became a stutterer; he remained almost mute until the age of fifteen. Jones graduated from the University of Michigan with a degree in drama; shortly thereafter he starred on Broadway in a production of *Othello*.

With his forceful presence, he caught the eye of director Stanley Kubrick, who cast him in *Dr. Strangelove*. Jones' heart, however, was still in the theater, and he accepted a role in *The Great White Hope*, playing Jack Jefferson, a black prize fighter with a white mistress (Jane Alexander). He won a Tony Award for his performance, and joined most of the original Broadway cast in the movie version. For his portrayal of the arrogant, strong-willed Jefferson, Jones received a Golden Globe Award and was nominated for an Academy Award as Best Actor.

His commanding voice was in demand for documentaries, but his acting career was at a standstill. His career took off in the mid-seventies when he became the voice of the villainous Darth Vadar in the *Star Wars* trilogy.

Jones won another Tony in 1987 for his performance in August Wilson's *Fences*. In 1988, he starred as a J. D. Salinger-like author in *Field of Dreams*. Subsequent film credits include *Gardens of Stone, Matewan, Coming to America, The Hunt for Red October, Patriot Games, Sneakers, Clear and Present Danger, Jefferson in Paris, Cry, the Beloved Country, A Family Thing, The Lion King* and *Looking for Richard.*

Jones' series television credits include *Homicide: Life on the Street, Frasier, Touched by an Angel* and a starring role in *Gabriel's Fire.* Recent telefilms include *The Second Civil War, Rebound* and *What the Deaf Man Heard* (Hallmark Hall of Fame).

MIRANDA RICHARDSON (Mab, Lady of the Lake) is one of the most versatile actresses working today, receiving accolades for her work in film, television and on stage. A native of Lancashire, England, she originally aspired to be a veterinary surgeon, but then decided to study drama and was accepted by the Bristol Old Vic Theatre School. Graduation was followed by several years of repertory theater. While playing in *The Life of Einstein* at the Duke's Playhouse in Lancaster, director Mike Newell cast her as Ruth Ellis, the last woman to be hanged in England, in *Dance with a Stranger.* Although not a box office success, the film garnered her several British film awards and brought Richardson to the attention of Steven Spielberg, who cast her in his epic, *Empire of the Sun.* Many films followed, including *Enchanted April* (1992), for which she received her first Golden Globe Award (Best Actress in a Comedy), Neil Jordan's controversial *The Crying Game* (1992), *Damage* (1992, Oscar nomination—Best Actress), *Tom and Viv* (1994, Academy Award and Golden Globe nominations—Best Actress), *Robert Altman's Kansas City* (1996) and *The Evening Star* (1996).

Richardson's television career has been equally rich. She has starred in many British television films, as well as the popular British comedy *Blackadder* and the miniseries *A Woman of Substance.* She also had a memorable turn on the hugely successful BBC comedy *Absolutely Fabulous,* playing Bettina. Richardson received her third Golden Globe nomination (and second award—Best Actress in a Miniseries) for her performance in *Fatherland* (1995).

ISABELLA ROSSELLINI (Nimue) began her career before the camera as a broadcast journalist for RAI-Italian Television. At the relatively advanced age of twenty-eight, she became a model, working with photographers such as Richard Avedon, Helmut Newton, Peter Lindburgh and Steven Meisel. For fourteen years she was the exclusive spokesmodel for Lancôme cosmetics.

Rossellini's American film debut was opposite Mikhail Baryshnikov and Gregory Hines in Taylor Hackford's *White Nights* (1985). In 1986, she starred opposite Dennis Hopper as Dorothy Vallens, the tortured lounge singer, in David Lynch's haunting and controversial *Blue Velvet*. Other films include the romantic comedy *Cousins* (opposite Ted Danson) and *Wild at Heart* (also from David Lynch). In 1992, she was featured in *Death Becomes Her*, opposite Meryl Streep, Goldie Hawn and Bruce Willis, and *Fearless*, opposite Jeff Bridges and Rosie Perez. She starred as Big Nose Kate in Lawrence Kasdan's *Wyatt Earp* (opposite Kevin Costner and Dennis Quaid), and in *Immortal Beloved* with Gary Oldman. Most recently, Rossellini starred as a two-timing girlfriend in *Big Night*, co-directed by Stanley Tucci and Campbell Scott, which won Best Screenplay at the 1996 Sundance Film Festival; and in Abel Ferrara's *The Funeral*.

For television, Rossellini starred as the goddess Athena in last season's NBC/Hallmark Entertainment miniseries *The Odyssey*. She has appeared in *The Last Elephant* (opposite John Lithgow), *The Frightening Frammis* (starring Peter Gallagher) and *The Gift* (Laura Dern's directorial debut). She guested on the critically acclaimed *The Tracey Ullman Show*, and starred in Robert Zemeckis' *You Murderer*, again opposite John Lithgow. Other recent television roles were the wife of accused Lindburgh baby kidnapper Bruno Hauptmann (Stephen Rea) in *Crime of the Century*, for which she received a Golden Globe nomination as Best Actress; a guest stint as herself on an episode of NBC's *Friends;* and a two episode arc of *Chicago Hope*, for which she received an Emmy nomination.

This past summer, Rossellini's self-described fictional memoir was published, titled *Some of Me* (Random House).

MARTIN SHORT (Frik) has been acclaimed a comic genius since his first appearances on Canadian television in *SCTV*. A native of Hamilton, Ontario, Short was majoring in social work at McMaster University when he secured a role in his first professional production, *Godspell*. Other theatrical work followed, leading to his selection as a member of Toronto's famed Second City comedy troupe. In 1984, Short joined the cast of NBC's *Saturday Night Live,* and American audiences were introduced to such hilarious characters as Ed Grimley, Jackie Rogers Jr., legendary Tin Pan Alley songwriter Irving Cohen and ethically-challenged lawyer Nathan Thurm.

While at *Saturday Night Live,* Short made his feature-film debut opposite Steve Martin and Chevy Chase in *Three Amigos*. Other films include *Innerspace, Cross My Heart, The Big Picture* (with Kevin Bacon), *Clifford, Captain Ron* (opposite Kurt Russell) and two turns as the unforgettable wedding and baby planner, Franck, in *Father of the Bride* and *Father of the Bride 2* (both with Steve Martin and Diane Keaton). Short's recent films include Tim Burton's *Mars Attacks, Jungle 2 Jungle* (with Tim Allen) and *A Simple Wish* (with Kathleen Turner). He will also voice one of the characters in the first animated film from DreamWorks, *The Prince of Egypt*.

In the last several years, Short has written, produced and starred in three highly acclaimed comedy specials: *Martin Short's Concert for the North Americas* (CableACE Award), *I, Martin Short Goes Hollywood* (CableACE Award) and *The Show Formerly Known as the Martin Short Show* (Emmy Award).

In 1994, Short was awarded the Order of Canada (the Canadian equivalent of British knighthood) by the Canadian government.

ROBERT HALMI, SR. (Executive Producer) was born in Budapest, Hungary, in 1924. His exploits with the Hungarian Resistance during World War II formed the basis of the film, *Trial by Terror*.

While perhaps best known for the resounding success of NBC's Emmy-winning miniseries *Gulliver's Travels*, and last season's *The Odyssey*, Halmi has had a varied and successful career in photography, documentary filmmaking and as a film and television producer. He emigrated to the United States in 1950, became a photographer for Life magazine and published eleven books on subjects as diverse as African wildlife, world zoos and sports cars. He made his first films in the 1960s, including thirteen seasons of *Outdoors with Liberty Mutual*.

By the mid-1970s Halmi had gravitated towards feature films and television dramas; his fifty-plus credits include *Svengali* (Peter O'Toole, Jodie Foster), *Terrible Joe Moran* (James Cagney), *Izzy and Moe* (Jackie Gleason, Art Carney), *Barnum* (Burt Lancaster), *Bump in the Night* (Christopher Reeve, Meredith Baxter), *The Josephine Baker Story* (five Emmy Awards), *Mr. and Mrs. Bridge* (Paul Newman, Joanne Woodward), *The Secret* (Kirk Douglas), *Gypsy* (Bette Midler), *Lonesome Dove* (six Emmy Awards) and the Hallmark Hall of Fame presentations *Face to Face, Pack of Lies, April Morning, An American Story* and *Blind Spot*.

In 1994, Halmi sold his company (RHI) to Hallmark Cards. The newly created Hallmark Entertainment, of which he is chairman, is the world's leading supplier of movies and miniseries for television. Recent high-profile projects include *Streets of Laredo* (James Garner, Sissy Spacek, Sam Shepard), *Bye Bye Birdie* (Jason Alexander, Vanessa Williams, Chynna Phillips), Neil Simon's *Jake's Women* (Alan Alda, Anne Archer) and *London Suite* (Kelsey Grammer, Julia Louis-Dreyfus, Michael Richards, Kristen Johnston), *In Cold Blood* (Anthony Edwards, Eric Roberts) and the aforementioned *Gulliver's Travels* (Ted Danson, Mary Steenburgen) and *The Odyssey* (Armand Assante, Isabella Rossellini, Greta Scacchi).

DYSON LOVELL (Producer) also produced last season's *The Odyssey,* and has produced feature films and television movies in England and the U.S. for over twenty years. Born in Rhodesia, he studied acting at the Royal Academy of Dramatic Art and subsequently joined the Old Vic Theatre Company. After casting and assistant directing Franco Zeffirelli's *Romeo and Juliet,* he was a production executive with James Bond producers Harry Saltzman and Cubby Broccoli, and at EMI, where he put together the packages for four Agatha Christie films, including *Murder on the Orient Express* and *Death on the Nile.*

His feature film producing credits include *Jane Eyre,* with Charlotte Gainsbourg and William Hurt; Zeffirelli's *Hamlet,* with Mel Gibson and Glenn Close; Francis Ford Coppola's *The Cotton Club* (executive producer); *Endless Love;* and *The Champ.* He produced the television movies *Nobody's Child* and the award-winning miniseries *Lonesome Dove.*

CAST AND CREW CREDITS

Sunday and Monday, April 26 and 27, 1998
(9-11 p.m. ET)
A Hallmark Entertainment production for NBC

MERLIN

Sam Neill, Isabella Rossellini, Miranda Richardson, Martin Short,
Rutger Hauer, Helena Bonham Carter, John Gielgud, James Earl Jones

Executive Producer
Robert Halmi, Sr.

Directed by Steve Barron

Produced by Dyson Lovell

Teleplay by David Stevens
and Peter Barnes;
Story by Ed Khmara

Music by Trevor Jones

Editor Colin Green

Production Designer
Roger Hall

Director of Photography
Sergei Kozlov

Costume Designer
Ann Hollowood

Casting Director (U.S.)
Lynn Kressel

Casting Director (U.K.)
Noel Davis

Visual Effects,
Supervising Designer &
Second Unit Director
Tim Webber

Creature Effects by Jim
Henson's Creature Shop

Computer-Generated
Images (CGI) by FrameStore

CAST

Player	Role	Player	Role
Sam Neill	Merlin	Billie Whitelaw	Ambrosia
Isabella Rossellini	Nimue	Timothy Bateson	Father Abbott
Miranda Richardson	Mab/Lady of the Lake	Dilys Lane	Gudrun
Martin Short	Frik	Emma Lewis	Elissa
Rutger Hauer	Vortigern	Talula Sheppard	Lady Friend
Helena Bonham Carter	Morgan Le Fey	Peter Benson	First Architect
John Gielgud	King Constant	Peter Woodthorpe	Soothsayer
James Earl Jones	Mountain King	John Tordoff	New Architect
Paul Curran	Arthur	Robert Addie	Sir Gilbert
Jeremy Sheffield	Lancelot	Nickolas Grace	Sir Egbert
Lena Heady	Guinevere	Janine Eser	Lady Elaine
Mark Jax	King Uther	Alice Hamilton	Young Morgan Le Fey
John McEnery	Lord Ardent	Jeremy Peters	Village Chief
Thomas Lockyer	Duke of Cornwall	Joseph Mawle	Village Man
Roger Ashton-Griffiths	Sir Boris	Peter Eyre	Chief Physician
Rachel Colover	Lady Igraine	Vernon Dobtcheff	First Physician
John Turner	Lord Lot	Camilla Oultram	Young Girl at Fair
Keith Baxter	Sir Hector	Daniel Brocklebank	Young Merlin
Nicholas Clay	Lord Leo	Agnieszka Koson	Young Nimue
Justin Gurdler	Galahad	Peter Baylis	Second Physician
Sebastian Roche	Gawain	Susan Rayner	Village Woman
Jason Done	Mordred	Charlotte Church	Singer